WISE WORDS
FROM ACROSS
SPACE AND TIME

BBC *The Official Quotable*
DOCTOR WHO

Cavan Scott and Mark Wright

**HARPER
DESIGN**
An Imprint of HarperCollins Publishers

Text © Cavan Scott and Mark Wright, 2014
Illustrations by Ben Morris © Woodlands Books Ltd, 2014

Doctor Who is a BBC Wales production for BBC One.
Executive Producers: Steven Moffat and Brian Minchin

HarperCollins books may be purchased for educational, business, or sales promotional use.
For information please e-mail the Special Markets Department at SPsales@harpercollins.com.

First published in 2014 by:
Harper Design
An Imprint of HarperCollins*Publishers*
195 Broadway
New York, NY 10007
Tel: (212) 207-7000
Fax: (212) 207-7654

Distributed throughout the world by:
HarperCollins*Publishers*
195 Broadway
New York, NY 10007

Library of Congress Number: 2014935024
ISBN 978-0-06-233614-9

Commissioning editor: Albert DePetrillo
Editorial manager: Lizzy Gaisford
Series consultant: Justin Richards
Project editor: Steve Tribe
Illustrations: Ben Morris Illustration
Design: Seagull Design
Production: Alex Goddard

Printed and bound in the United States.

16 17 LP/RRD 13 12 11 10 9 8 7

CONTENTS

INTRODUCTION

'I'm a Time Lord. I've been around, you know. Two hearts, respiratory bypass system. I haven't lived seven hundred and fifty years without learning something…'

THE DOCTOR, *THE ROBOTS OF DEATH*

Have you ever wondered what it would be like to travel with the Doctor, have you? To be wanderers in the fourth dimension?

All that running. All those corridors. All those monsters.

They say that travel broadens the mind, in which case the Doctor's mind must be the broadest of them all. Over a thousand years of rattling around the universe in his big blue box… Imagine all the wisdom he's gathered in his meanderings, all the lessons he's learnt.

Perhaps that would be the best part of jumping on board the TARDIS – having the greatest tour guide in all of history. He shows you the big stuff, the galaxies and planets and constellations, but the small things too. The simple things. A pretty painting. A stupid joke. A cup of tea and a jammy dodger. Real life in all its wonder and whimsy.

The good news is that we can travel with the Doctor, and his friends and enemies too. We have been since 23 November

1963. He's taken us from a junkyard at the end of a lane to the end of time – and back again.

And there are lessons to be found in his adventures too. Some serious. Some silly. Some profound. Some potty. And more fezzes than you'd expect.

In many ways, this has been a nightmarish task. Cherry-picking the Doctor's best quotes, quips and sayings from over fifty years of adventures? The man never shuts up – and nor do his friends. Long may that continue.

For all this we must thank and pay homage to a select group, because first came the word. We would like to dedicate this compendium to the scriptwriters of *Doctor Who*; those wits and wise men and women who have toiled late into the night over typewriters and word processors. Across half a century they have put words in the mouths of the Doctor, his companions, friends and enemies. Their desire to tell a rattling good adventure yarn, their quick humour, their outlook on life, the universe and everything, have all given life and sparkle to the words we hear on screen – then taken the rest of the way by those brilliant actors. And let's not forget the script editors who kept them on the straight and narrow, provided guidance and contributed their own words of wonder. The quality and sheer inventiveness of their work has always set *Doctor Who* apart from other TV shows, and that is what we are celebrating in the pages of this book.

And the stories keep coming.

Brigadier Alistair Gordon Lethbridge-Stewart once told his daughter that science leads. He said he learnt it from an old friend.

What will the same old friend teach you today? Or tomorrow? Or maybe even yesterday? It's all a bit timey-wimey, to be honest.

Happy Times and Places!

Chapter One:
The Doctor

'I suppose you might say that
I am a citizen of the universe,
and a gentleman to boot.'

THE DOCTOR, *THE DALEKS' MASTER PLAN*

FAMOUS FIRST WORDS

'What are you doing here?'

THE FIRST DOCTOR, *AN UNEARTHLY CHILD*

'Slower... Slower... Concentrate on one thing. One thing!'

THE SECOND DOCTOR, *THE POWER OF THE DALEKS*

'Shoes... Must find my shoes.'

THE THIRD DOCTOR, *SPEARHEAD FROM SPACE*

'… typical Sontaran attitude… stop Linx… perverting the course of human history… I tell you, Brigadier, there's nothing to worry about. The brontosaurus is large and placid… and stupid! If the square on the hypotenuse equals the sum of the squares on the other two sides, why is a mouse when it spins? Never did know the answer to that one.'

THE FOURTH DOCTOR, *ROBOT*

'I… oh.'

THE FIFTH DOCTOR, *CASTROVALVA*

'You were expecting someone else?'

THE SIXTH DOCTOR, T*HE CAVES OF ANDROZANI*

'Oh no, Mel. Ah, that was a nice nap. Now, down to business.'

THE SEVENTH DOCTOR, *TIME AND THE RANI*

'Who am I? Who am I?'

THE EIGHTH DOCTOR, *DOCTOR WHO* (TV MOVIE)

'Doctor no more.'

THE WAR DOCTOR, *THE NIGHT OF THE DOCTOR*

'Run!'

THE NINTH DOCTOR, *ROSE*

'Hello. OK – oh. New teeth. That's weird. So, where was I? Oh, that's right. Barcelona.'

THE TENTH DOCTOR, *THE PARTING OF THE WAYS*

'Legs. Still got legs, good!! Arms. Hands. Ooh, fingers. Lots of fingers. Ears, yes. Eyes, two. Nose, I've had worse. Chin, blimey. Hair. I'm a girl! No. No, I'm not a girl. And still not ginger. And something else. Something important. I'm, I'm, I'm… Crashing! Geronimo!'

THE ELEVENTH DOCTOR, *THE END OF TIME*

'Kidneys! I've got new kidneys. I don't like the colour.'

THE TWELFTH DOCTOR, *THE TIME OF THE DOCTOR*

THE NAME OF THE DOCTOR

'Eh? Doctor who? What's he talking about?'

THE DOCTOR, *AN UNEARTHLY CHILD*

'I'm the Doctor. Well, they call me the Doctor. I don't know why. I call me the Doctor, too. Still don't know why.'

THE DOCTOR, *THE LODGER*

'You may be *a* doctor, but I'm *the* Doctor. The definite article, you might say.'

THE DOCTOR, *ROBOT*

CLARA: Doctor who?

THE DOCTOR: Oh, dangerous question.

CLARA: What's wrong with dangerous?

THE SNOWMEN

THE DOCTOR: I help where I can. I will not fight.

OHILA: Because you are 'the good man' as you call yourself?

THE DOCTOR: I call myself the Doctor.

OHILA: It's the same thing in your mind.

THE DOCTOR: I'd like to think so.

THE NIGHT OF THE DOCTOR

ADELAIDE BROOKE: State your name, rank and intention.

THE DOCTOR: The Doctor. Doctor. Fun.

THE WATERS OF MARS

TYRUM: We are grateful to you, human, for saving Voga.

THE DOCTOR: Oh, please, don't call me human. Just Doctor will do very nicely, thank you.

REVENGE OF THE CYBERMEN

THE DOCTOR: Doctor von Wer, at your service.

SERGEANT: Doctor who?

THE DOCTOR: That's what I said.

THE HIGHLANDERS

THE DOCTOR: I'm just Lord President of the Supreme Council of Time Lords on Gallifrey.

STOR: Your description fits that of one called Doctor.

THE DOCTOR: Well, that's not my fault. I'm Lord President, and I'm called 'sir'.

THE INVASION OF TIME

MADGE: Are you the new caretaker?

THE DOCTOR: Usually called the Doctor. Or the Caretaker or Get Off This Planet. Though, strictly speaking, that probably isn't a name.

THE DOCTOR, THE WIDOW AND THE WARDROBE

'Look, three options. One, I let the Star Whale continue in unendurable agony for hundreds more years. Two, I kill everyone on this ship. Three, I murder a beautiful, innocent creature as painlessly as I can. And then I find a new name, because I won't be the Doctor any more.'

THE DOCTOR, *THE BEAST BELOW*

'The name I chose is the Doctor. The name you choose, it's like a promise you make. He's the one who broke the promise.'

THE DOCTOR, ON THE WAR DOCTOR, *THE NAME OF THE DOCTOR*

'You haven't seen the last of me. Bad Penny is my middle name. Seriously, the looks I get when I fill in a form...'

THE DOCTOR, *THE GOD COMPLEX*

'Great men are forged in fire. It is the privilege of lesser men to light the flame, whatever the cost.'

THE WAR DOCTOR, *THE DAY OF THE DOCTOR*

'You've been asking a question, and it's time someone told you you've been getting it wrong. His name, his name is the Doctor. All the name he needs. Everything you need to know about him.'

CLARA, *THE TIME OF THE DOCTOR*

THE TRUTH OF THE MATTER

'I never lie. Well, hardly ever.'

THE DOCTOR, *THE TIME WARRIOR*

'Rule one. The Doctor lies.'

THE DOCTOR, *LET'S KILL HITLER*

WHO IS THE DOCTOR?

'I'm the Doctor. I'm a Time Lord. I'm from the planet Gallifrey in the constellation of Kasterborous. I'm nine hundred and three years old. And I'm the man that's going to save your lives and all six billion people on the planet below. You got a problem with that?'

THE DOCTOR, *VOYAGE OF THE DAMNED*

LUX: Who is the Doctor?

RIVER: The only story you'll ever tell, if you survive him.

FOREST OF THE DEAD

'They call me the Doctor. I am a scientist, an engineer. I'm a builder of things.'

THE DOCTOR, *THE AZTECS*

'I'm just a traveller, wandering past. Believe it or not, all I'm after is a quiet life.'

THE DOCTOR, *BAD WOLF*

'He saves planets, rescues civilisations, defeats terrible creatures. And runs a lot. Seriously, there's an outrageous amount of running involved.'

DONNA, *THE DOCTOR'S DAUGHTER*

EARL: You're a nice guy, Doctor, but a little weird.

THE DOCTOR: Enough of the little.

THE HAPPINESS PATROL

'Do you know like we were saying about the Earth revolving? It's like when you were a kid. The first time they tell you the world's turning and you just can't quite believe it because everything looks like it's standing still. I can feel it. The turn of the Earth. The ground beneath our feet is spinning at a thousand miles an hour, and the entire planet is hurtling round the sun at 67,000 miles an hour, and I can feel it. We're falling through space, you and me, clinging to the skin of this tiny little world, and if we let go… That's who I am.'

THE DOCTOR, *ROSE*

THE BRIGADIER: Sir, this is the Doctor, our scientific adviser.

GENERAL FINCH: Oh. We've been waiting for you, you know. May I ask where you've been?

THE DOCTOR: Certainly.

GENERAL FINCH: Well?

THE DOCTOR: You can ask but I don't guarantee that you'll get a reply.

INVASION OF THE DINOSAURS

'He's like fire and ice and rage. He's like the night and the storm in the heart of the sun… He's ancient and forever. He burns at the centre of time and he can see the turn of the universe… And he's wonderful.'

TIM LATIMER, *THE FAMILY OF BLOOD*

THE DOCTOR: I'm a Time Lord. A man of science, temperament and passion!

PERI: And a very loud voice.

ATTACK OF THE CYBERMEN

'I have lived a long life and I have seen a few things. I walked away from the Last Great Time War. I marked the passing of the Time Lords. I saw the birth of the universe and I watched as time ran out, moment by moment, until nothing remained. No time. No space. Just me. I walked in universes where the laws of physics were devised by the mind of a mad man. I've watched universes freeze and creations burn. I've seen things you wouldn't believe. I have lost things you will never understand. And I know things. Secrets that must never be told. Knowledge that must never be spoken.'

THE DOCTOR, *THE RINGS OF AKHATEN*

'Oh, he's like a rubber ball. He'll come bouncing out of there soon, full of ideas.'

BARBARA, *MARCO POLO*

ADELAIDE BROOKE: You the doctor or the janitor?

THE DOCTOR: I don't know. Sounds like me. The maintenance man of the universe.

THE WATERS OF MARS

'I've got a friend who specialises in trouble. He dives in and usually finds a way.'

IAN, *THE ROMANS*

'Some fifty years ago, I knew a man who solved the insoluble by the strangest means. He sees the threads that join the universe together and mends them when they break.'

ZASTOR, *MEGLOS*

ROSE: I can see everything. All that is, all that was, all that ever could be.

THE DOCTOR: That's what I see. All the time. And doesn't it drive you mad?

THE PARTING OF THE WAYS

'I'm not a human being. I walk in eternity.'

THE DOCTOR, *PYRAMIDS OF MARS*

'Whatever you've got planned, forget it. I'm the Doctor. I'm nine hundred and four years old. I'm from the planet Gallifrey in the constellation of Kasterborous. I am the Oncoming Storm, the Bringer of Darkness, and... you are basically just a rabbit, aren't you? OK, carry on. Just a general warning.'

THE DOCTOR, *THE DAY OF THE DOCTOR*

THE DOCTOR'S NATURE

'There is so much, so much to see, Amy. Because it goes so fast. I'm not running away from things, I am running to them before they flare and fade for ever.'

THE DOCTOR, *THE POWER OF THREE*

SARAH: Whatever's in that Tower, it's got enormous powers and, well, what can we do against it?

THE DOCTOR: What I've always done, Sarah Jane. Improvise.

THE FIVE DOCTORS

'I never take life. Only when my own is immediately threatened.'

THE DOCTOR, *THE DALEK INVASION OF EARTH*

KLIEG: But, how did you know in the first place?

THE DOCTOR: Oh, I use my own special technique.

KLIEG: Oh really, Doctor? And may we know what that is?

THE DOCTOR: Keeping my eyes open and my mouth shut.

THE TOMB OF THE CYBERMEN

'He is not a man to side with chaos.'

NEFRED, *FULL CIRCLE*

'I am and always will be the optimist. The hoper of far-flung hopes and dreamer of improbable dreams.'

THE DOCTOR, *THE ALMOST PEOPLE*

PALMERDALE: Are you in charge here?

THE DOCTOR: No, but I'm full of ideas.

HORROR OF FANG ROCK

'Oh, I always like to do the unexpected. Takes people by surprise.'

THE DOCTOR, *THE TRIAL OF A TIME LORD: THE MYSTERIOUS PLANET*

'So is this how it works, Doctor? You never interfere in the affairs of other peoples or planets, unless there's children crying?'

AMY, *THE BEAST BELOW*

VINCENT: You're not armed.

THE DOCTOR: I am.

VINCENT: What with?

THE DOCTOR: Overconfidence…and a small screwdriver. I'm absolutely sorted.

VINCENT AND THE DOCTOR

'I'd better get going. Things to do, worlds to save, swings to swing on.'

THE DOCTOR, *THE POWER OF THREE*

'He was the most alive person I ever met.'

SARAH, *THE MONSTER OF PELADON*

THE DOCTOR: You're going to fire me at a planet? That's your plan? I get fired at a planet and expected to fix it.

RORY: In fairness, that is slightly your MO.

ASYLUM OF THE DALEKS

'I hate being patient. Patience is for wimps. I can't live like this. Don't make me. I need to be busy.'

THE DOCTOR, *THE POWER OF THREE*

'The Eye of Orion's restful, if you like restful. I can never really get the hang of restful.'

THE DOCTOR, *THE DOCTOR'S WIFE*

'What's the point in two hearts, if you can't be a bit forgiving, now and then?'

THE DOCTOR, *DAY OF THE MOON*

'I've got one of those faces. People never stop blurting out their plans while I'm around.'

THE DOCTOR, *THE LODGER*

'Don't worship me – I'd make a very bad god. You wouldn't get a day off, for starters.'

THE DOCTOR, *BOOM TOWN*

THE DOCTOR: I'll be back for you soon as I can, I promise.

AMY: You always say that.

THE DOCTOR: I always come back.

FLESH AND STONE

'Something's interfering with time, Mr Scarman, and time is *my* business.'

THE DOCTOR, *PYRAMIDS OF MARS*

CAPTAIN COOK: I wonder you manage to explore anything. Everything seems to alarm you so.

THE DOCTOR: Not everything. I trust my instincts, and you may recall they're not always wrong.

THE GREATEST SHOW IN THE GALAXY

'But Doctor, listen to me. Don't get emotional because that's when you make mistakes.'

AMY, *THE DOCTOR'S WIFE*

CRAIG: Has anyone ever told you that you're a bit weird?

THE DOCTOR: They never really stop.

THE LODGER

'Doctor, the more you try to convince me that you're a fool, the more I'm likely to think otherwise.'

THE COUNTESS, *CITY OF DEATH*

'Why do I always let my curiosity get the better of me?'

THE DOCTOR, *BLACK ORCHID*

'I'm always serious. With days off.'

THE DOCTOR, *COLD WAR*

THE COUNTESS: My dear, I don't think he's as stupid as he seems.

SCARLIONI: My dear, nobody could be as stupid as *he* seems.

CITY OF DEATH

'Interfere? Of course we should interfere. Always do what you're best at, that's what I say.'

THE DOCTOR, *NIGHTMARE OF EDEN*

BARBARA: Doctor, I thought we were never going to see you again.

THE DOCTOR: You should know by now, young lady, that you can't get rid of the old Doctor as easily as that.

THE REIGN OF TERROR

QUALIFICATIONS

'The Doctor is not weaponless. He has the greatest weapon of all. Knowledge.'

CAMILLA, *STATE OF DECAY*

'The Doctor's qualified to do almost everything.'

THE BRIGADIER, *DOCTOR WHO AND THE SILURIANS*

THE DOCTOR: I am the Doctor.

ENLIGHTENMENT: A doctor? Of what?

THE DOCTOR: Of everything.

FOUR TO DOOMSDAY

'My colleague is a doctor of medicine and I'm a doctor of many things.'

THE DOCTOR, *REVENGE OF THE CYBERMEN*

'I'm every kind of scientist.'

THE DOCTOR, *COLONY IN SPACE*

BORUSA: You make me regret teaching you anything at all.

THE DOCTOR: You taught me nothing. Nothing that instinct couldn't provide better.

THE INVASION OF TIME

'I am not a student of human nature. I am a professor of a far wider academy, of which human nature is merely a part.'

THE DOCTOR, *THE EVIL OF THE DALEKS*

ZONDAL: You do not look like a scientist.

THE DOCTOR: Well, looks aren't everything, you know.

THE ICE WARRIORS

NEFRED: You understand a great deal, Doctor.

THE DOCTOR: True.

NEFRED: But not everything.

THE DOCTOR: That's certainly true.

FULL CIRCLE

MODESTY

OVERSEER: I suppose you think you're very clever.

THE DOCTOR: Well, without any undue modesty, yes!

THE REIGN OF TERROR

'Your leader will be angry if you kill me. I'm a genius.'

THE DOCTOR, *THE SEEDS OF DEATH*

IAN: You're a genius.

THE DOCTOR: Yes, there are very few of us left.

THE DALEK INVASION OF EARTH

THE DOCTOR: Jamie, some of the most brilliant scientists in the universe have assembled here to work together in pure research. I don't want them to know that I've arrived.

JAMIE: Why not?

THE DOCTOR: Think of the commotion! They'll all be scrambling around wanting my autograph.

THE TWO DOCTORS

CANTON: You, sir, are a genius.

THE DOCTOR: It's a hobby.

THE IMPOSSIBLE ASTRONAUT

SERGEANT: I'm sorry, sir, you're not allowed in there.

THE DOCTOR: Not allowed? Me? I'm allowed everywhere.

THE FIVE DOCTORS

THE DOCTOR: So you're just about an expert in everything except the things in your museum. Anything you don't understand, you lock up.

VAN STATTEN: And you claim greater knowledge?

THE DOCTOR: I don't need to make claims, I know how good I am.

DALEK

'I can feel my hair curling, and that means either it's going to rain or else I'm on to something.'

THE DOCTOR, *THE DEADLY ASSASSIN*

'This is magnificent. And I don't often say that because... well, because of me.'

THE DOCTOR, *UTOPIA*

ROSE: You think you're so impressive.

THE DOCTOR: I am so impressive.

ROSE: You wish.

THE END OF THE WORLD

'Oh, you know, K-9, sometimes I think I'm wasted just rushing around the universe saving planets from destruction. With a talent like mine, I might have been a great slow bowler.'

THE DOCTOR, *THE HORNS OF NIMON*

'Well, to be fair, I did have a couple of gadgets which he probably didn't, like a teaspoon and an open mind.'

THE DOCTOR, *THE CREATURE FROM THE PIT*

THE DOCTOR: Well, you'd better introduce me.

ROMANA: As what?

THE DOCTOR: Oh, I don't know, a sort of wise and wonderful person who wants to help. Don't exaggerate.

THE POWER OF KROLL

THE DOCTOR: I think my idea's better.

LESTER: What is your idea?

THE DOCTOR: I don't know yet. That's the trouble with ideas. They only come a bit at a time.

REVENGE OF THE CYBERMEN

'This is a situation that requires tact and finesse. Fortunately, I am blessed with both.'

THE DOCTOR, *THE TRIAL OF A TIME LORD: TERROR OF THE VERVOIDS*

'Look, it's perfectly understandable. I go zooming around space and time, saving planets, fighting monsters and being well, let's be honest, pretty sort of marvellous, so naturally now and then people notice me.'

THE DOCTOR, *TIME CRASH*

IAN: You know, Doctor, sometimes you astound me.

THE DOCTOR: Only sometimes, dear boy?

THE DALEK INVASION OF EARTH

'I have the directional instincts of a homing pigeon.'

THE DOCTOR, *THE CHASE*

CHASE: What do you do for an encore, Doctor?

THE DOCTOR: I win.

THE SEEDS OF DOOM

'Well, you can't expect perfection, you know. Not even from me.'

THE DOCTOR, *THE FACE OF EVIL*

ROMANA: You are incredible.

THE DOCTOR: Yes, I suppose I am, really. I've never given it much thought.

STATE OF DECAY

THE AGE OF THE DOCTOR

'Back when I first started at the very beginning, I was always trying to be old and grumpy and important, like you do when you're young.'

THE DOCTOR, *TIME CRASH*

'There is something new in you, yet something older than the sky itself.'

JOANNA, *THE CRUSADE*

SHAKESPEARE: How can a man so young have eyes so old?

THE DOCTOR: I do a lot of reading.

THE SHAKESPEARE CODE

THE DOCTOR: I've lived for something like seven hundred and fifty years.

SARAH: Oh, you'll soon be middle aged.

THE DOCTOR: Yes!

PYRAMIDS OF MARS

'I'm called the Doctor. Date of birth difficult to remember. Sometime quite soon, I think.'

THE DOCTOR, *NIGHTMARE OF EDEN*

'I'm afraid I'm much too old to be a pioneer. Although I was once amongst my own people.'

THE DOCTOR, *THE DALEKS*

'Oi! Listen, mush. Old eyes, remember? I've been around the block a few times. More than a few. They've knocked down the blocks I've been round and rebuilt them as bigger blocks. Super blocks. And I've been round them as well.'

THE DOCTOR, *NIGHT TERRORS*

'Can't remember if I'm lying about my age, that's how old I am.'

THE DOCTOR, *THE DAY OF THE DOCTOR*

LIFE WITH THE DOCTOR

MICKEY: Is this like normal for you? Is this an average day?

ROSE: Life with the Doctor, Mickey? No more average days.

THE GIRL IN THE FIREPLACE

'When I say run, run.'

THE DOCTOR, *THE EVIL OF THE DALEKS*

'It's the way it's always been. The monsters and the Doctor. It seems you cannot have one without the other.'

REINETTE, *THE GIRL IN THE FIREPLACE*

ROMANA: You nearly got us killed.

THE DOCTOR: If you call that being nearly killed, you haven't lived yet. Just stay with me and you'll get a lot nearer.

THE RIBOS OPERATION

'Trouble seems to follow you, doesn't it, Doctor?'

THE BRIGADIER, *INFERNO*

'I don't work for anybody. I'm just having fun.'

THE DOCTOR, *NIGHTMARE OF EDEN*

'This is my life, Jackie. It's not fun, it's not smart. It's just standing up and making a decision because nobody else will.'

THE DOCTOR, *WORLD WAR THREE*

THE DOCTOR: The situation's worse than you imagine.

PERI: It always is.

THE TRIAL OF A TIME LORD: THE MYSTERIOUS PLANET

CLARA: Doctor, what are you going to do?

THE DOCTOR: Oh, I don't know. Talk very fast, hope something good happens, take the credit. That's generally how it works.

THE TIME OF THE DOCTOR

'If I knew everything that was going to happen, where would the fun be?'

THE DOCTOR, *THE KEEPER OF TRAKEN*

'I mean, this is what he does, Jacks, that Doctor bloke. Every where he goes, death and destruction, and he's got Rose in the middle of it.'

MICKEY, *WORLD WAR THREE*

'Oh, I must be mad. I'm sick of being cold and wet, and hypnotised left right and centre. I'm sick of being shot at, savaged by bug-eyed monsters, never knowing if I'm coming or going or been.'

SARAH, *THE HAND OF FEAR*

'As long as he does the job, he can wear what face he likes.'

THE BRIGADIER, *THE THREE DOCTORS*

'Wish I'd never met you, Doctor. I was much better off as a coward.'

CAPTAIN JACK HARKNESS, *THE PARTING OF THE WAYS*

'Flying the TARDIS was always easy. It was flying the Doctor I never quite mastered.'

TASHA LEM, *THE TIME OF THE DOCTOR*

'When you run with the Doctor, it feels like it will never end. But however hard you try, you can't run for ever. Everybody knows that everybody dies, and nobody knows it like the Doctor. But I do think that all the skies of all the worlds might just turn dark, if he ever, for one moment, accepts it.'

RIVER SONG, *FOREST OF THE DEAD*

'I'd hate to have to live my life by some boring old rulebook like you do.'

THE DOCTOR, *PARADISE TOWERS*

ROSE: He thought you were brilliant.

DONNA: Don't be stupid.

ROSE: But you are. It just took the Doctor to show you that, simply by being with him. He did the same to me. To everyone he touches.

TURN LEFT

BRIAN: Go save every world you can find. Who else has that chance? Life will still be here.

THE DOCTOR: You could come, Brian.

BRIAN: Somebody's got to water the plants.

THE POWER OF THREE

LIFE WITHOUT THE DOCTOR

'You were my life. You know what the most difficult thing was? Coping with what happens next, or with what doesn't happen next. You took me to the furthest reaches of the galaxy, you showed me supernovas, intergalactic battles, and then you just dropped me back on Earth. How could anything compare to that? … We get a taste of that splendour and then we have to go back.'

SARAH, *SCHOOL REUNION*

'It's life. Just life. That thing that goes on when you're not there.'

AMY, *ASYLUM OF THE DALEKS*

AMY: After everything we've been through, Doctor. Everything. You can't just drop me off at my house and say goodbye like we've shared a cab.

THE DOCTOR: And what's the alternative? Me standing over your grave?

THE GOD COMPLEX

'Our lives won't run the same. They can't. One day, soon maybe, you'll stop. I've known for a while.'

THE DOCTOR TO AMY, *THE POWER OF THREE*

CRITICISING THE DOCTOR

'Don't trust him. There's a sliver of ice in his heart.'

EMMA, *HIDE*

CLARA: I trust the Doctor.

CAPTAIN: You think he knows what he's doing?

CLARA: I'm not sure I'd go that far.

NIGHTMARE IN SILVER

'Oh yes. I'm only his assistant. He's the one you should be talking to. Or rather, listening to, if you have the stamina.'

ROMANA, *THE PIRATE PLANET*

HARRIET: Excuse me, people are dead! This is not the time for making jokes.

ROSE: Sorry. You get used to this stuff when you're friends with him.

HARRIET: Well, that's a strange friendship.

WORLD WAR THREE

COMMODORE TRAVERS: If I seem to lack gratitude, young woman … it is because on the previous occasion that the Doctor's path crossed mine I found myself involved in a web of mayhem and intrigue.

THE DOCTOR: Ah, saved your ship though, Commodore.

COMMODORE TRAVERS: Yes, you did, though whether it would have been at risk without your intervention is another matter.

THE TRIAL OF A TIME LORD: TERROR OF THE VERVOIDS

'Don't listen to me. I never do.'

THE DOCTOR, *THE KEEPER OF TRAKEN*

VIVIEN: I'm sure the Doctor's perfectly capable of looking after himself.

ROMANA: I'm not sure I'd entirely agree with that remark.

THE STONES OF BLOOD

'The Doctor. The man who keeps running, never looking back because he dare not, out of shame. This is my final victory, Doctor. I have shown you yourself.'

DAVROS, *JOURNEY'S END*

'You know what's going on … You always know. You just can't be bothered to tell anyone. It's like it's some kind of a game, and only you know the rules.'

ACE, *THE CURSE OF FENRIC*

'How like a man to have fun while there's disaster all around him.'

AGATHA CHRISTIE, *THE UNICORN AND THE WASP*

'It's funny, you know, but before I met you, I was even willing to be impressed … Of course, now I realise that your behaviour simply derives from a sub-transitory, experiential hypertoid-induced condition, aggravated, I expect, by multi-encephalogical tensions … to put it very simply, Doctor, you're suffering from a massive compensation syndrome.'

ROMANA, *THE RIBOS OPERATION*

'The Doctor has no idea of time. For someone who's travelled about in time as much as he has, that's rather funny.'

DODO, *THE SAVAGES*

'Call yourself a Time Lord? A broken clock keeps better time than you do. At least it's accurate twice a day, which is more than you ever are.'

TEGAN, *THE VISITATION*

ROMANA: I told you you'd got the time wrong, Doctor.

THE DOCTOR: Yes, but you're always saying that.

ROMANA: You're always getting the time wrong.

SHADA

ROMANA: Is that why you always win?

THE DOCTOR: Yes. What?

ROMANA: Because you always make mistakes.

THE DOCTOR: Mistakes? Me? Well, perhaps once a century or so.

DESTINY OF THE DALEKS

JOSIAH: You're so smug and self-satisfied, Doctor.

THE DOCTOR: I try.

GHOST LIGHT

THE DARK SIDE OF THE DOCTOR

'I'm so old now. I used to have so much mercy. You get one warning. That was it.'

THE DOCTOR, *SCHOOL REUNION*

'The Doctor is a legend woven throughout history. When disaster comes, he's there. He brings the storm in his wake and he has one constant companion … Death.'

CLIVE, *ROSE*

'You look deep enough on the internet or in the history books, and there's his name, followed by a list of the dead.'

MICKEY, *ALIENS OF LONDON*

'Every time the Doctor gets pally with someone, I have this overwhelming urge to notify their next of kin.'

RORY, *THE GOD COMPLEX*

'Answer me this. Just one question, that's all. If the Doctor had never visited us, if he'd never chosen this place on a whim, would anybody here have died?'

JOAN, *THE FAMILY OF BLOOD*

'No, you've noticed something. You've got your noticing face on. I have nightmares about that face.'

CRAIG, *CLOSING TIME*

'The man who abhors violence, never carrying a gun. But this is the truth, Doctor. You take ordinary people, and you fashion them into weapons. Behold your Children of Time. Transformed into murderers. I made the Daleks, Doctor. You made this.'

DAVROS, *JOURNEY'S END*

'Good men don't need rules. Today is not the day to find out why I have so many.'

THE DOCTOR, *A GOOD MAN GOES TO WAR*

'You know what's dangerous about you? It's not that you make people take risks, it's that you make them want to impress you. You make it so they don't want to let you down. You have no idea how dangerous you make people to themselves when you're around.'

RORY, *VAMPIRES OF VENICE*

'I don't know what you are, the two of you, or where you're from, but I know that you consort with stars and magic and think it fun. But your world is steeped in terror and blasphemy and death, and I will not allow it. You will leave these shores and you will reflect, I hope, on how you came to stray so far from all that is good, and how much longer you may survive this terrible life. Now leave my world, and never return.'

QUEEN VICTORIA, *TOOTH AND CLAW*

'You gave me hope, and then you took it away. That's enough to make anyone dangerous. God knows what it will do to me. Basically, run!'

THE DOCTOR, *THE DOCTOR'S WIFE*

JOHN SMITH: You're this Doctor's companion. Can't you help? What exactly do you do for him? Why does he need you?

MARTHA: Because he's lonely.

THE FAMILY OF BLOOD

'You've got an unconscious death wish.'

ROMANA, *THE RIBOS OPERATION*

'You know, Stephen King said once, he said, salvation and damnation are the same thing. And I never knew what he meant. But I do now, because the Doctor might be wonderful, but thinking back, I was having such a special time. Just for a bit. I had this nice little gang, and they were destroyed. It's not his fault, but maybe that's what happens if you touch the Doctor. Even for a second. I keep thinking of Rose and Jackie. And how much longer before they pay the price.'

ELTON, *LOVE & MONSTERS*

'Falling in love? That didn't even occur to him? ... Then what sort of man is that?'

JOHN SMITH, *THE FAMILY OF BLOOD*

THE DOCTOR: You've seen it out there. It's beautiful.

DONNA: And it's terrible. That place was flooding and burning and they were dying, and you were stood there like, I don't know, a stranger. And then you made it snow. I mean, you scare me to death.

THE RUNAWAY BRIDE

'Just promise me one thing. Find someone ... Because sometimes, I think you need someone to stop you.'

DONNA, *THE RUNAWAY BRIDE*

'I choose my friends with great care. Otherwise, I'm stuck with my own company, and you know how that works out.'

THE DOCTOR, *AMY'S CHOICE*

'People have died. The Daleks are all over the place, fit to murder the lot of us, and all you can say is you've had a good night's work.'

JAMIE, *THE EVIL OF THE DALEKS*

'I'm the Doctor. And if you don't like it, if you want to take it to a higher authority, then there isn't one. It stops with me.'

THE DOCTOR, *NEW EARTH*

'He never raised his voice. That was the worst thing. The fury of the Time Lord. And then we discovered why. Why this Doctor, who had fought with gods and demons, why he'd run away from us and hidden. He was being kind.'

SON OF MINE, *THE FAMILY OF BLOOD*

'When you began, all those years ago, sailing off to see the universe, did you ever think you'd become this? The man who can turn an army around at the mention of his name. Doctor. The word for healer and wise man throughout the universe. We get that word from you, you know. But if you carry on the way you are, what might that word come to mean? To the people of the Gamma Forests, the word Doctor means mighty warrior. How far you've come. And now they've taken a child, the child of your best friends, and they're going to turn her into a weapon just to bring you down. And all this, my love, in fear of you.'

RIVER SONG, *A GOOD MAN GOES TO WAR*

'If he's singled you out, if the Doctor's making house calls, then God help you.'

CLIVE, *ROSE*

'From what I've seen, your funny little happy-go-lucky life leaves devastation in its wake. Always moving on because you dare not look back. Playing with so many people's lives, you might as well be a god.'

MARGARET BLAINE, *BOOM TOWN*

THE ONCOMING STORM

'Do you know what they call me in the ancient legends of the Dalek Homeworld? The Oncoming Storm. You might've removed all your emotions but I reckon right down deep in your DNA, there's one little spark left, and that's fear. Doesn't it just burn when you face me?'

THE DOCTOR, *THE PARTING OF THE WAYS*

'I'm a dead man. I knew that as soon as I came through that door, so you'd better watch out. You see, I've nothing to lose, have I?'

THE DOCTOR, *THE DAEMONS*

'You have the mouth of a prattling jackanapes, but your eyes – they tell a different story.'

SHARAZ JEK, *THE CAVES OF ANDROZANI*

THE DOCTOR: Even monsters from under the bed have nightmares, don't you, monster?

YOUNG REINETTE: What do monsters have nightmares about?

THE DOCTOR: Me!

THE GIRL IN THE FIREPLACE

'His entire history is one of opposition to conquest. While he lives, he is a threat.'

CHEDAKI, *THE ANDROID INVASION*

'The Doctor is never more dangerous than when the odds are against him.'

THE MASTER, *THE DEADLY ASSASSIN*

'Didn't anyone ever tell you there's one thing you never put in a trap? If you're smart, if you value your continued existence, if you have any plans about seeing tomorrow, there is one thing you never, ever put in a trap: Me.'

THE DOCTOR, *THE TIME OF ANGELS*

VASTRA: The Doctor has been many things, but never blood-soaked.

DR SIMEON: Tell that to the leader of the Sycorax, or Solomon the trader, or the Cybermen, or the Daleks. The Doctor lives his life in darker hues, day upon day, and he will have other names before the end. The Storm, the Beast, the Valeyard.

THE NAME OF THE DOCTOR

'Just remember who's standing in your way. Remember every black day I ever stopped you, and then, and then, do the smart thing. Let somebody else try first.'

THE DOCTOR, *THE PANDORICA OPENS*

'The way I see it, every life is a pile of good things and bad things. Hey. The good things don't always soften the bad things, but vice versa, the bad things don't necessarily spoil the good things or make them unimportant.'

THE DOCTOR, *VINCENT AND THE DOCTOR*

THE DOCTOR AND HIS COMPANIONS

'I only take the best.'

THE DOCTOR, *THE LONG GAME*

'How do you do? Have you met Miss Smith? She's my best friend.'

THE DOCTOR, *THE SEEDS OF DOOM*

'The Doctor sort of travels through time and space and picks people up. God, I make us sound like stray dogs. Maybe we are.'

MARTHA, *UTOPIA*

'I've seen a lot of this universe. I've seen fake gods and bad gods and demi-gods and would-be gods, and out of all that, out of that whole pantheon, if I believe in one thing, just one thing, I believe in her.'

THE DOCTOR ON ROSE, *THE SATAN PIT*

BARBARA: We worked upwards from the three Rs ... Reading, writing, 'rithmetic.

VICKI: Oh, it was a nursery school.

BARBARA: It was not!

THE WEB PLANET

'I'm being extremely clever up here, and there's no one to stand around looking impressed! What's the point in having you all?'

THE DOCTOR, *THE IMPOSSIBLE ASTRONAUT*

THE VALEYARD: I have calculated on a random Matrix sample that the Doctor's companions have been placed in danger twice as often as the Doctor.

THE DOCTOR: Well, there have been many companions, but only one me.

THE TRIAL OF A TIME LORD: MINDWARP

'Anything you have to say to me, you can say in front of Clara. Well, quite a lot of it. Probably about half. Maybe a smidge under. Actually, Clara, would you mind waiting out here, please?'

THE DOCTOR, *THE TIME OF THE DOCTOR*

SARAH: What you're trying to say is that you're busy and you'd like us to push off.

THE DOCTOR: I'd phrase it more elegantly myself, of course. But yes.

THE SONTARAN EXPERIMENT

ROSE: You're not keeping the horse.

THE DOCTOR: I let you keep Mickey.

THE GIRL IN THE FIREPLACE

'Exotic alien swords are easy to come by. Aces are rare.'

THE DOCTOR, *BATTLEFIELD*

'What you need, Doctor, as Miss Shaw herself so often remarked, is someone to pass you your test tubes and to tell you how brilliant you are. Miss Grant will fulfil that function admirably.'

THE BRIGADIER, *TERROR OF THE AUTONS*

THE DOCTOR: Sarah. What are you doing here?

SARAH: Rescuing you, actually. For a change.

THE ANDROID INVASION

'Well, look round. Ask questions. People like it when you're with a baby. Babies are sweet. People talk to you. That's why I usually take a human with me.'

THE DOCTOR, *CLOSING TIME*

DONNA: I'm sorry. I'm going home.

THE DOCTOR: Really? … I had so many places I wanted to take you. The fifteenth broken moon of the Medusa Cascade. The lightning skies of Cotter Palluni's World. Diamond coral reefs of Kataa Flo Ko. Thank you. Thank you, Donna Noble. It's been brilliant. You've… you've saved my life in so many ways. You're… you're just popping home for a visit, that's what you mean.

DONNA: You dumbo.

THE SONTARAN STRATAGEM

ROMANA: My name is Romanadvoratrelundar.

THE DOCTOR: I'm so sorry about that. Is there anything we can do?

THE RIBOS OPERATION

'Is that why you travel round with a human at your side? It's not so you can show them the wonders of the universe, it's so you can take cheap shots?'

DONNA, *PLANET OF THE OOD*

ROMANA: I don't like 'Romana'.

THE DOCTOR: It's either 'Romana' or 'Fred'.

ROMANA: All right, call me 'Fred'.

THE DOCTOR: Good. Come on, Romana.

THE RIBOS OPERATION

'Your mind is beginning to work. It's entirely due to my influence, of course. You mustn't take any credit.'

THE DOCTOR TO HARRY, *THE ARK IN SPACE*

'Do you think that for once in your life you could manage to arrive before the nick of time?'

THE DOCTOR TO THE BRIGADIER, *THE MIND OF EVIL*

STEVEN: You know, I'm beginning to like the idea of being a crewmember on a time machine.

VICKI: A crewmember? You'll be lucky. He's the crew. We're just the passengers.

THE TIME MEDDLER

THE DOCTOR: I wanted to see how you were. You know me, I don't just abandon people when they leave the TARDIS. This Time Lord's for life. You don't get rid of your old pal, the Doctor, so easily.

AMY: Hmm. You came here by mistake, didn't you?

THE DOCTOR: Yeah, bit of a mistake.

AMY'S CHOICE

THE DOCTOR: How do you feel now?

TEGAN: Groggy, sore and bad-tempered.

THE DOCTOR: Oh, almost your old self.

THE VISITATION

THE DOCTOR: Well, come on, old girl. There's quite a few millennia left in you yet.

ROMANA: Thank you, Doctor.

THE DOCTOR: Not you, the TARDIS.

THE HORNS OF NIMON

'Sometimes I do worry about you, though. I think once we're gone, you won't be coming back here for a while, and you might be alone, which you should never be. Don't be alone, Doctor.'

AMY, *THE ANGELS TAKE MANHATTAN*

FAMILY

ROSE: He's your dad.

TOMMY: He's an idiot.

ROSE: Of course he is. Like I said, he's your dad.

THE IDIOT'S LANTERN

'Weak and strong. It's a translation. Translated from the base code of nature itself. You and I, Cyril, we're weak. But she's female. More than female, she's Mum. How else does life ever travel? The Mother ship.'

THE DOCTOR, *THE DOCTOR, THE WIDOW AND THE WARDROBE*

'There isn't a little boy born who wouldn't tear the world apart to save his mummy. And this little boy can.'

THE DOCTOR, *THE DOCTOR DANCES*

'Your dad's trying his best, you know. Yes, I know it's not his fault he doesn't have mammary glands. No, neither do I.'

THE DOCTOR, *CLOSING TIME*

'Nine hundred years of time and space, and I've never been slapped by someone's mother.'

THE DOCTOR, *ALIENS OF LONDON*

'Oh, who needs family? I've got the whole world on my shoulders.'

THE DOCTOR, *THE AGE OF STEEL*

ROSE: This is my fault.

PETE: No, love. I'm your dad. It's my job for it to be my fault.

FATHER'S DAY

THE DOCTOR: My dear girl, the one purpose in growing old is to accumulate knowledge and wisdom, and to help other people.

SUSAN: So I'm to be treated like a silly little child.

THE DOCTOR: If you behave like one, yes.

THE SENSORITES

'You're a mother, aren't you … There's kindness in your eyes. And sadness, but a ferocity too.'

KAHLER-JEX TO AMY, *A TOWN CALLED MERCY*

DROXIL: There's nothing you could say that would convince me you'd ever use that gun.

MADGE: Oh really? Well, I'm looking for my children.

THE DOCTOR, THE WIDOW AND THE WARDROBE

THE DOCTOR: I just want you to know there are worlds out there, safe in the sky because of her. That there are people living in the light, and singing songs of Donna Noble, a thousand million light years away. They will never forget her, while she can never remember. And for one moment, one shining moment, she was the most important woman in the whole wide universe.

SYLVIA: She still is. She's my daughter.

THE DOCTOR: Then maybe you should tell her that once in a while.

JOURNEY'S END

CRAIG: Yes, I meant on my own with the baby. Yes. Because no one thinks I can cope on my own. Which is so unfair, because I can't cope on my own with him. I can't. He just cries all the time. I mean, do they have off switches?

THE DOCTOR: Human beings? No. Believe me, I've checked.

CLOSING TIME

VICTORIA: You probably can't remember your family.

THE DOCTOR: Oh yes, I can when I want to. And that's the point, really. I have to really want to, to bring them back in front of my eyes. The rest of the time they sleep in my mind, and I forget.

THE TOMB OF THE CYBERMEN

HAPPINESS

'Build high for happiness.'

THE KANGS, *PARADISE TOWERS*

'I think it does us good to be reminded the universe isn't entirely peopled with nasty creatures out for themselves.'

THE DOCTOR, *CASTROVALVA*

'Happiness will prevail.'

HELEN A, *THE HAPPINESS PATROL*

'You want moves, Rose? I'll give you moves. Everybody lives, Rose. Just this once, everybody lives!'

THE DOCTOR, *THE DOCTOR DANCES*

PEACE AND UNDERSTANDING

'As we learn about each other, so we learn about ourselves.'

THE DOCTOR, *THE EDGE OF DESTRUCTION*

'Mankind doesn't need warfare and bloodshed to prove itself. Everyday life can provide honour and valour, and let's hope that from now on this, this country can find its heroes in smaller places.'

JOHN SMITH, *HUMAN NATURE*

THE DOCTOR: I could rule the universe with this, Chancellor.

BORUSA: Is that what you want? Destroy that gun. Destroy all knowledge of it. It'll throw us back to the darkest age!

SONTARAN: No, Chancellor, forward.

THE INVASION OF TIME

WATSON: They're the most powerful missiles we have.

THE DOCTOR: On your standards, perhaps. I think we should try much older weapons… Speech. Diplomacy … Conversation.

THE HAND OF FEAR

MARSHAL: We must have the weapon that will wipe the Zeons clear of our skies once and for all. Can you provide it?

THE DOCTOR: Yes, I think so.

MARSHAL: What is it?

THE DOCTOR: Peace.

THE ARMAGEDDON FACTOR

'Some days are special. Some days are so, so blessed. Some days, nobody dies at all. Now and then, every once in a very long while, every day in a million days, when the wind stands fair, and the Doctor comes to call, everybody lives.'

RIVER SONG, *FOREST OF THE DEAD*

BRAVERY

'Brave heart, Tegan.'

THE DOCTOR, *EARTHSHOCK*

DESTROYER: Pitiful. Can this world do no better than you as their champion?

THE BRIGADIER: Probably. I just do the best I can.

BATTLEFIELD

'Unless we are prepared to sacrifice our lives for the good of all, then evil and anarchy will spread like the plague.'

THE DOCTOR, *THE TRIAL OF A TIME LORD: THE ULTIMATE FOE*

'It was a better life. And I don't mean all the travelling and seeing aliens and spaceships and things. That don't matter. The Doctor showed me a better way of living your life. You know, he showed you too. That you don't just give up. You don't just let things happen. You make a stand. You say no. You have the guts to do what's right when everyone else just runs away, and I just can't.'

ROSE, *THE PARTING OF THE WAYS*

OCTAVIAN: I will die in the knowledge that my courage did not desert me at the end. For that I thank God, and bless the path that takes you to safety.

THE DOCTOR: I wish I'd known you better.

OCTAVIAN: I think, sir, you know me at my best.

FLESH AND STONE

'I've a young friend on the Beacon. Sarah Jane, the girl who was here. She risked her life to save mine. The least I can do is accept the same risk for her.'

THE DOCTOR, *REVENGE OF THE CYBERMEN*

'Courage isn't just a matter of not being frightened, you know… It's being afraid and doing what you have to do anyway.'

THE DOCTOR, *PLANET OF THE DALEKS*

THE DOCTOR: I'm going to save Rose Tyler from the middle of the Dalek fleet. And then I'm going to save the Earth, and then, just to finish off, I'm going to wipe every last stinking Dalek out of the sky!

DALEK: But you have no weapons, no defences, no plan.

THE DOCTOR: Yeah. And doesn't that scare you to death.

BAD WOLF

TRUTH

JENNY: Madame Vastra will ask you questions. You will confine yourself to single-word responses. One word only, do you understand?

CLARA: Why?

VASTRA: Truth is singular. Lies are words, words, words.

THE SNOWMEN

'For a lie to work, madam, it must be shrouded in truth.'

THE MASTER, *THE TRIAL OF A TIME LORD: THE ULTIMATE FOE*

'I have the two qualities you require to see absolute truth. I am brilliant, and unloved.'

MISS EVANGELISTA, *FOREST OF THE DEAD*

'The very powerful and the very stupid have one thing in common. They don't alter their views to fit the facts. They alter the facts to fit their views. Which can be uncomfortable if you happen to be one of the facts that needs altering.'

THE DOCTOR, *THE FACE OF EVIL*

'Only in mathematics will we find truth.'

THE DOCTOR, QUOTING BORUSA, *THE DEADLY ASSASSIN*

FRIENDSHIP

'If it's time to go, remember what you're leaving. Remember the best. My friends have always been the best of me.'

THE DOCTOR, *THE WEDDING OF RIVER SONG*

THE DOCTOR: I imagine you'd prefer to be alone.

MADGE: I don't believe anyone would prefer that.

THE DOCTOR, THE WIDOW AND THE WARDROBE

DONNA: That Martha must've done you good.

THE DOCTOR: She did, yeah. Yeah. She did. She fancied me.

DONNA: Mad Martha, that one. Blind Martha. Charity Martha.

PARTNERS IN CRIME

'People fall out of the world sometimes, but they always leave traces. Little things we can't quite account for. Faces in photographs, luggage, half-eaten meals. Rings. Nothing is ever forgotten, not completely. And if something can be remembered, it can come back.'

THE DOCTOR, *THE PANDORICA OPENS*

'You were there for me when I had a bad day. Always like to return a favour. Got a bit glitchy in the middle there, but it sort of worked out in the end. Story of my life.'

THE DOCTOR, *THE DOCTOR, THE WIDOW AND THE WARDROBE*

LOVE

'Love has never been known for its rationality.'

THE DOCTOR, *DELTA AND THE BANNERMEN*

MARRINER: Without you I am nothing… I am empty. You give me being. I look into your mind and see life, energy, excitement. I want them. I want you. Your thoughts should be my thoughts. Your feelings, my feelings.

TEGAN: Wait a minute. Are you trying to tell me you're in love?

MARRINER: Love? What is love? I want existence.

ENLIGHTENMENT

'Love and hate, frightening feelings, especially when they're trapped struggling beneath the surface.'

THE DOCTOR, *THE CURSE OF FENRIC*

'You know when sometimes you meet someone so beautiful and then you actually talk to them, and five minutes later they're as dull as a brick? Then there's other people, and you meet them and you think, not bad, they're OK. And then you get to know them, and their face just sort of becomes them, like their personality's written all over it. And they just turn into something so beautiful.'

AMY, *THE GIRL WHO WAITED*

'I'm going to pull time apart for you.'

AMY, *THE GIRL WHO WAITED*

AMY: I love you, too. Don't let me in. Tell Amy, your Amy, I'm giving her the days. The days with you. The days to come.

RORY: I'm so, so sorry.

AMY: The days I can't have. Take them, please. I'm giving you my days.'

THE GIRL WHO WAITED

CRAIG: The Cybermen. They blew up. I blew them up with love.

THE DOCTOR: No, that's impossible. And also grossly sentimental and over-simplistic. You destroyed them because of the deeply ingrained hereditary human trait to protect one's own genes, which in turn triggered a... a... a... Yeah. Love. You blew them up with love.

CLOSING TIME

'Better a broken heart than no heart at all.'

THE DOCTOR, *A CHRISTMAS CAROL*

FLIRTING

THE DOCTOR: My dear boy, I could kiss you!

BARBARA: Don't waste it on him, kiss me instead!

THE CHASE

JACKIE: I'm in my dressing gown.

THE DOCTOR: Yes, you are.

JACKIE: There's a strange man in my bedroom.

THE DOCTOR: Yes, there is.

JACKIE: Well, anything could happen.

THE DOCTOR: No.

ROSE

LAZARUS: That's an interesting perfume. What's it called?

TISH: Soap.

THE LAZARUS EXPERIMENT

TASHA: Is that a new body? Give us a twirl.

THE DOCTOR: Tush, this old thing? Please, I've been rocking it for centuries.

THE TIME OF THE DOCTOR

ROSE: OK, so he's vanished into thin air. Why is it always the great-looking ones who do that?

THE DOCTOR: I'm making an effort not to be insulted.

ROSE: I mean, men.

THE DOCTOR: OK, thanks, that really helped.

THE DOCTOR DANCES

'The thrill is in the chase, never in the capture.'

AGATHA CHRISTIE, *THE UNICORN AND THE WASP*

THE BRIGADIER: You may not have noticed, but I'm a bit old-fashioned myself.

SARAH: Oh, nonsense, Brigadier. You're a swinger.

ROBOT

JABE: The gift of peace. I bring you a cutting of my grandfather.

THE DOCTOR: Thank you. Yes, gifts. Er, I give you in return air from my lungs.

JABE: How intimate.

THE DOCTOR: There's more where that came from.

JABE: I bet there is.

THE END OF THE WORLD

THE DOCTOR: I just want a mate.

DONNA: You just want to mate?

THE DOCTOR: I just want *a* mate!

DONNA: You're not mating with me, sunshine!

PARTNERS IN CRIME

'He saved my life. Bloke-wise, that's up there with flossing.'

ROSE, *THE DOCTOR DANCES*

HAWTHORNE: Sergeant, we must do the fertility dance to celebrate.

BENTON: Oh, no, I'm sorry, ma'am. I'm still rather busy.

THE DAEMONS

THE DOCTOR: Your boss, you should just ask her out. She likes you... She said that you were a Mister Hottie-ness, and that she would like to go out with you for texting and scones.

RORY: You really haven't done this before, have you?

THE DOCTOR: No, I haven't.

THE WEDDING OF RIVER SONG

RORY: There are soldiers all over my house, and I'm in my pants.

AMY: My whole life I've dreamed of saying that, and I miss it by being someone else.

THE POWER OF THREE

'My lonely Doctor. Dance with me... There comes a time, Time Lord, when every lonely little boy must learn how to dance.'

REINETTE, *THE GIRL IN THE FIREPLACE*

CLARA: Do you think I'm pretty?

THE DOCTOR: No. You're too short and bossy, and your nose is all funny.

NIGHTMARE IN SILVER

'Nine hundred years old, me. I've been around a bit. I think you can assume at some point I've danced.'

THE DOCTOR, *THE DOCTOR DANCES*

'This is how it all ends. Pond flirting with herself. True love at last.'

THE DOCTOR, *TIME*

THE DOCTOR: Do you mind flirting outside?

JACK: I was just saying hello!

THE DOCTOR: For you, that's flirting.

BAD WOLF

ROSE: You just handed me a piece of paper telling me you're single and you work out.

JACK: Tricky thing, psychic paper.

ROSE: Yeah. Can't let your mind wander when you're handing it over.

THE EMPTY CHILD

THE DOCTOR: We were talking about dancing.

JACK: It didn't look like talking.

ROSE: It didn't feel like dancing.

THE DOCTOR DANCES

K-9: She is prettier than you, master.

THE DOCTOR: Is she? What's that got to do with it?

THE PIRATE PLANET

KISSING

'A Zygon, yes. Big red rubbery thing covered in suckers. Surprisingly good kisser.'

THE DOCTOR, THE DAY OF THE DOCTOR

'You're never short of a snog with an extra head.'

THE DOCTOR, *THE TIME OF ANGELS*

KAZRAN: I've never kissed anyone before. What do I do?

THE DOCTOR: Try and be all nervous and rubbish and a bit shaky... Because you're going to be like that anyway. Might as well make it part of the plan, then it'll feel on purpose... Trust me. It's this or go to your room and design a new kind of screwdriver. Don't make my mistakes.

A CHRISTMAS CAROL

RORY: Of course I've got a job. What do you think we do when we're not with you?

THE DOCTOR: I imagined mostly kissing.

THE POWER OF THREE

'We've all got to go some time. There are worse ways than having your face snogged off by a dodgy mermaid.'

THE DOCTOR, *THE CURSE OF THE BLACK SPOT*

JACKIE: What do you need?

THE DOCTOR: Anything with vinegar!

JACKIE: Gherkins. Yeah, pickled onions. Pickled eggs.

THE DOCTOR: And you kiss this man?

WORLD WAR THREE

'Biting's excellent. It's like kissing, only there's a winner.'

IDRIS, *THE DOCTOR'S WIFE*

THE DOCTOR: She kissed me.

RORY: And you kissed her back.

THE DOCTOR: No. I kissed her mouth.

THE VAMPIRES OF VENICE

THE WAR DOCTOR: Is there a lot of this in the future?

THE DOCTOR: It does start to happen, yeah.

THE DAY OF THE DOCTOR

RELATIONSHIPS

'I dated a Nestene duplicate once. Swappable head. It did keep things fresh.'

RIVER SONG, *THE BIG BANG*

'You think you know us so well, Doctor. But we're not abandoned. Not while we have each other.'

BRANNIGAN, *GRIDLOCK*

THE BRIGADIER: Oh dear. Women. Not really my field.

THE DOCTOR: Don't worry, Brigadier. People will be shooting at you soon.

BATTLEFIELD

IAN: Where did you get hold of this?

THE DOCTOR: My fiancée.

IAN: I see. Your what?

THE DOCTOR: Yes, I made some cocoa and got engaged.

THE AZTECS

'I don't care that you got old. I care that we didn't grow old together.'

RORY, *THE GIRL WHO WAITED*

CLARA: Emergency. You're my boyfriend.

THE DOCTOR: Ding dong. OK, brilliant. I may be a bit rusty in some areas, but I will glance at a manual.

THE TIME OF THE DOCTOR

KAZRAN: When girls are crying, are you supposed to talk to them?

THE DOCTOR: I have absolutely no idea.

A CHRISTMAS CAROL

RORY: Amy, I thought I'd lost you.

AMY: What, cause I was sucked into the ground? You're so clingy.

COLD BLOOD

'Let me tell you something about those who get left behind. Because it's hard. And that's what you become, hard. But if there's one thing I've learnt, it's that I will never let her down. And I'll protect them both until the end of my life. So whatever you want, I'm warning you, back off.'

JACKIE TYLER, *LOVE & MONSTERS*

'Sometimes it's like I've lived a thousand lives in a thousand places. I'm born, I live, I die. And always, there's the Doctor. Always I'm running to save the Doctor again and again and again... And he hardly ever hears me. But I've always been there.'

CLARA, *THE NAME OF THE DOCTOR*

'It's the oldest story in the universe, this one or any other. Boy and girl fall in love, get separated by events. War, politics, accidents in time. She's thrown out of the hex, or he's thrown into it. Since then they've been yearning for each other across time and space, across dimensions. This isn't a ghost story, it's a love story!'

THE DOCTOR, *HIDE*

'Hold hands. That's what you're meant to do. Keep doing that and don't let go. That's the secret.'

THE DOCTOR, *HIDE*

THE MOST COMPLICATED RELATIONSHIP OF THEM ALL

'Hello Sweetie!'

RIVER SONG, *SILENCE IN THE LIBRARY*

CHURCHILL: What's she like? Attractive, I assume.

THE DOCTOR: Hell, in high heels.

CHURCHILL: Tell me more.

THE WEDDING OF RIVER SONG

'You know when you see a photograph of someone you know, but it's from years before you knew them and it's like they're not quite finished. They're not done yet. Well, yes, the Doctor's here. He came when I called, just like he always does. But not my Doctor. Now *my* Doctor, I've seen whole armies turn and run away. And he'd just swagger off back to his TARDIS and open the doors with a snap of his fingers. The Doctor in the TARDIS. Next stop, everywhere.'

RIVER SONG, *FOREST OF THE DEAD*

THE DOCTOR: River Song, I could bloody kiss you.

RIVER: Ah well, maybe when you're older.

FLESH AND STONE

'It was never going to be a gun for you, Doctor. The man of peace who understands every kind of warfare, except, perhaps, the cruellest.'

RIVER SONG, *LET'S KILL HITLER*

THE DOCTOR: Doctor Song, you've got that face on again.

RIVER: What face?

THE DOCTOR: The 'he's hot when he's clever' face.

RIVER: This is my normal face.

THE DOCTOR: Yes, it is.

RIVER: Oh, shut up.

THE IMPOSSIBLE ASTRONAUT

RIVER: I'd trust that man to the end of the universe. And actually, we've been.

ANITA: He doesn't act like he trusts you.

RIVER: Yeah, there's a tiny problem. He hasn't met me yet.

FOREST OF THE DEAD

'You, me, handcuffs. Must it always end this way?'

RIVER SONG, *FLESH AND STONE*

'It's a long story, Doctor. It can't be told, it has to be lived. No sneak previews.'

RIVER SONG, *FLESH AND STONE*

THE DOCTOR: Can I trust you, River Song?

RIVER: If you like. But where's the fun in that?

FLESH AND STONE

'Funny thing is, this means you've always known how I was going to die. All the time we've been together, you knew I was coming here. The last time I saw you, the real you, the future you, I mean, you turned up on my doorstep, with a new haircut and a suit. You took me to Darillium to see the Singing Towers. What a night that was. The Towers sang, and you cried.'

RIVER SONG, *FOREST OF THE DEAD*

RIVER: How are you even doing that? I'm not really here.

THE DOCTOR: You are always here to me. And I always listen, and I can always see you.

RIVER: Then why didn't you speak to me?

THE DOCTOR: Because I thought it would hurt too much.

RIVER: I believe I could have coped.

THE DOCTOR: No, I thought it would hurt me. And I was right.

THE NAME OF THE DOCTOR

LIVING LIFE TO THE FULL

'Living minds are contaminated with crude emotions, organic, irrational, creative, entertaining.'

THE DOCTOR, *ENLIGHTENMENT*

'There is no indignity in being afraid to die. But there is a terrible shame in being afraid to live.'

ALYDON, *THE DALEKS*

'If you're so desperate to stay alive, why don't you live a little?'

THE DOCTOR, *NEW EARTH*

'Letting it get to you. You know what that's called? Being alive. Best thing there is. Being alive right now, that's all that counts.'

THE DOCTOR, *THE DOCTOR'S WIFE*

Chapter Three:
The Darkness

'There are some corners of the universe which have bred the most terrible things. Things which act against everything that we believe in. They must be fought.'

THE DOCTOR, *THE MOONBASE*

LONELINESS

'You can spend the rest of your life with me, but I can't spend the rest of mine with you. I have to live on. Alone. That's the curse of the Time Lords.'

THE DOCTOR, *SCHOOL REUNION*

'They leave. Because they should. Or they find someone else. And some of them — some of them forget me. I suppose in the end… they break my heart.'

THE DOCTOR, *THE NEXT DOCTOR*

'If one's interest is held, loneliness does not exist.'

CAMECA, *THE AZTECS*

'I can't stand burnt toast. I loathe bus stations. Terrible places, full of lost luggage and lost souls.'

THE DOCTOR, *GHOST LIGHT*

SADNESS

'Children cry because they want attention, because they're hurt or afraid. But when they cry silently, it's because they just can't stop. Any parent knows that.'

THE DOCTOR, *THE BEAST BELOW*

'I know this great song about this bloke and his girlfriend. She drops the ring he gives her on the railway track, and when she goes back to get it, she's killed by the train and he's really miserable for the rest of his life. Oh, it's fantastic.'

ACE, *THE HAPPINESS PATROL*

SALLY: I love old things. They make me feel sad.

KATHY: What's good about sad?

SALLY: It's happy for deep people.

BLINK

'Happiness is nothing unless it exists side by side with sadness.'

THE DOCTOR, *THE HAPPINESS PATROL*

ENEMIES

'You can always judge a man by the quality of his enemies.'

THE DOCTOR, *REMEMBRANCE OF THE DALEKS*

'Do you know any nice people? You know, ordinary people, not power-crazed nutters trying to take over the galaxy?'

ACE, *SURVIVAL*

LEELA: It is fitting to celebrate the death of an enemy.

THE DOCTOR: Not in my opinion.

HORROR OF FANG ROCK

'If Hitler invaded hell, I would give a favourable reference to the Devil.'

WINSTON CHURCHILL, *VICTORY OF THE DALEKS*

'Am I addressing the Consciousness? … Thank you. If I might observe, you infiltrated this civilisation by means of warp-shunt technology. So, may I suggest, with the greatest respect, that you… shunt off?'

THE DOCTOR, *ROSE*

THE DOCTOR: Mrs Gillyflower, you have no idea what you are dealing with. In the wrong hands, that venom could wipe out all life on this planet.

MRS GILLYFLOWER: Do you know what these are? The wrong hands.

THE CRIMSON HORROR

'Only a fool defends his enemies.'

TEGANA, *MARCO POLO*

'You know, my dear, there's something very satisfying in destroying something that's evil, don't you think?'

THE DOCTOR, *THE SAVAGES*

'Your evil is my good. I am Sutekh the Destroyer. Where I tread I leave nothing but dust and darkness. I find that good.'

SUTEKH, *PYRAMIDS OF MARS*

FEAR

'Fear makes companions of all of us.'

THE DOCTOR, *AN UNEARTHLY CHILD*

'Don't run. Now, I know you're scared, but never run when you're scared.'

THE DOCTOR, *LET'S KILL HITLER*

HOUSE: Fear me. I've killed hundreds of Time Lords.

THE DOCTOR: Fear me. I've killed all of them.

THE DOCTOR'S WIFE

'Safe? No, of course you're not safe. There's about a billion other things out there just waiting to burn your whole world. But, if you want to pretend you're safe, just so you can sleep at night? OK, you're safe. But you're not really.'

THE DOCTOR, *DAY OF THE MOON*

'Some things are better left undone, and I have a feeling that this is one of them.'

THE DOCTOR, *THE TOMB OF THE CYBERMEN*

'You know when grown-ups tell you everything's going to be fine and you think they're probably lying to make you feel better? ... Everything's going to be fine.'

THE DOCTOR, *THE ELEVENTH HOUR*

'You must throw off these suspicions. They're based on fear, and fear breeds hatred and war.'

TEMMOSUS, *THE DALEKS*

RORY: I will take you apart cog by cog and melt you down when all this is over.

ROBOT 1: Oh, I'm so scared. Actually, I might be. A little bit of oil just came out.

DINOSAURS ON A SPACESHIP

'One only harms that which one fears.'

MONARCH, *FOUR TO DOOMSDAY*

'Fear itself is largely an illusion. And at my age, there's little left to fear.'

THE DOCTOR, *THE FIVE DOCTORS*

DEATH

'It all just disappears, doesn't it? Everything you are, gone in a moment, like breath on a mirror.'

THE DOCTOR, *THE TIME OF THE DOCTOR*

'It is never easy to die.'

STAEL, *IMAGE OF THE FENDAHL*

'All things pass away.'

CHO-JE, *PLANET OF THE SPIDERS*

'Death is always more frightening when it strikes invisibly.'

THE MASTER, *TERROR OF THE AUTONS*

'Since when did an undertaker keep office hours? The dead don't die on schedule.'

CHARLES DICKENS, *THE UNQUIET DEAD*

'The Church of the Papal Mainframe apologises for your death. The relevant afterlives have been notified.'

COLONEL ALBERO, *THE TIME OF THE DOCTOR*

RORY: What's wrong with you? What's she done to you?

THE DOCTOR: Poisoned me. But I'm fine. Well, no, I'm dying, but I've got a plan.

AMY: What plan?

THE DOCTOR: Not dying.

LET'S KILL HITLER

'With one basic difference, the living are very much like the dead. Who was it said the living are just the dead on holiday?'

THE DOCTOR, *DESTINY OF THE DALEKS*

'If Ben was killed by that damn blasted machine, there'll be anger in his soul. And men that die like that don't never rest easy.'

REUBEN, *HORROR OF FANG ROCK*

'That is the smell of death, Peri. Ancient musk, heavy in the air. Fruit-soft flesh, peeling from white bones. The unholy, unburiable smell of Armageddon. Nothing quite so evocative as one's sense of smell, is there?'

THE DOCTOR, *THE TWO DOCTORS*

'I'll expose him, ruin him, have him arrested, but I won't be his executioner. No one has that right.'

THE DOCTOR, *THE ENEMY OF THE WORLD*

THE DOCTOR: You know, the window's quite out of place. It's not in character at all.

ROMANA: Will you stop babbling about the architecture? We're having a serious conversation about death.

THE DOCTOR: Well, architecture's quite a serious subject.

THE POWER OF KROLL

'It doesn't end there. That is how it all begins again, with a killing. It doesn't end. That ends as it has always done, in chaos and despair. It ends as it begins, in the darkness. Is that what you all want?'

PANNA, *KINDA*

AMY: So, what's wrong with me?

RIVER: Nothing. You're fine.

THE DOCTOR: Everything. You're dying.

RIVER: Doctor!

THE DOCTOR: Yes, you're right. If we lie to her, she'll get all better.

FLESH AND STONE

'Welcome. You are unauthorised. Your death will now be implemented. Welcome. You will experience a tingling sensation and then death. Remain calm while your life is extracted.'

ANTIBODY, *LET'S KILL HITLER*

THE DOCTOR: I know a rogue when I see a rogue and I've no desire to die in the company of a rogue. Have you any desire to die in the company of a rogue?

ROMANA: I'd rather not die at all.

THE DOCTOR: I know that feeling.

THE POWER OF KROLL

THE DOCTOR: Alive isn't sad.

IDRIS: It's sad when it's over.

THE DOCTOR'S WIFE

'That's the charm of a ghost story, isn't it? Not the scares and chills, that's just for children, but the hope of some contact with the great beyond. We all want some message from that place. It's the Creator's greatest mystery that we're allowed no such consolation. The dead stay silent, and we must wait.'

QUEEN VICTORIA, *TOOTH AND CLAW*

DICKENS: This is precisely the sort of cheap mummery I strive to unmask. Séances? Nothing but luminous tambourines and a squeeze box concealed between the knees. This girl knows nothing.

THE DOCTOR: Now, don't antagonise her. I love a happy medium.

THE UNQUIET DEAD

'When it comes to death, quantity is so much more satisfying than quality.'

FENRIC, *THE CURSE OF FENRIC*

'You've been trying to kill me for centuries, and here I am, dying of old age. If you want something done, do it yourself.'

THE DOCTOR, *THE TIME OF THE DOCTOR*

WAR

'The universe is at war, Doctor. Name one planet whose history is not littered with atrocities and ambition for empire. It is a universal way of life.'

DAVROS, *RESURRECTION OF THE DALEKS*

'You don't beg for peace, Princess. You win it.'

MARSHAL, *THE ARMAGEDDON FACTOR*

CONSTANTINE: Before this war began, I was a father and a grandfather. Now I am neither. But I'm still a doctor.

THE DOCTOR: Yeah. I know the feeling.

THE EMPTY CHILD

'A warrior doesn't talk, he acts.'

STAAL, *THE POISON SKY*

'Sir, please do not noogie me during combat prep.'

STRAX, *THE SNOWMEN*

'It is the right of every creature across the universe to survive, multiply and perpetuate its species. How else does the predator exist? We are all predators, Doctor. We kill, we devour, to live. Survival is all, you agree?'

THE NUCLEUS, *THE INVISIBLE ENEMY*

TEGANA: In battle all men face death.

THE DOCTOR: And few expect to meet it, hmmm?

MARCO POLO

'A child is not a weapon!'

THE DOCTOR, *A GOOD MAN GOES TO WAR*

'It used to be the Tiberion Spiral Galaxy. A million star systems, a hundred million worlds, a billion trillion people. It's not there any more. No more Tiberion Galaxy. No more Cybermen. It was effective… I feel like a monster sometimes… Because instead of mourning a billion trillion dead people, I just feel sorry for the poor blighter who had to press the button and blow it all up.'

PORRIDGE, *NIGHTMARE IN SILVER*

'War, a game played by politicians. We were just pawns in the game, but the pawns are fighting together now.'

VERSHININ, *THE CURSE OF FENRIC*

'War is another world. You cannot apply the politics of peace to what I did. To what any of us did.'

KAHLER-JEX, *A TOWN CALLED MERCY*

'A heroic war cry to apparently peaceful ends is one of the greatest weapons a politician has.'

MAVIC CHEN, *THE DALEKS' MASTER PLAN*

'I killed, and I caused to have killed. I sent young men and women to their deaths, but here I am, still alive and it does tend to haunt you. Living, after so much of the other thing.'

PALMER, *HIDE*

'It is not patriotism to lead people into a war they cannot win.'

SELRIS, *THE KROTONS*

'Victory should be naked!'

JOSEPH GREEN, *WORLD WAR THREE*

'You're caught in an impasse of logic. You've discovered the recipe for everlasting peace. Congratulations. I'm terribly pleased.'

THE DOCTOR, *DESTINY OF THE DALEKS*

'What better way to destroy your enemies than to let them destroy themselves.'

IXTA, *THE AZTECS*

THE DOCTOR: They keep coming back, don't you see? Every time I negotiate, I try to understand. Well, not today. No. Today, I honour the victims first. His, the Master's, the Daleks', all the people who died because of my mercy!

AMY: You see, this is what happens when you travel alone for too long.

A TOWN CALLED MERCY

'Strategy is worth a hundred lances.'

SALADIN, *THE CRUSADE*

'You're a man for talk, I can see that. You like a table and a ring of men – a parley here, arrangements there. But when you men of eloquence have stunned each other with your words, we – we the soldiers – have to face it out. On some half-started morning while you speakers lie abed, armies settle everything, giving sweat, sinew, bodies, aye, and life itself.'

LORD LEICESTER, *THE CRUSADE*

AMY: We come in peace!

RORY: When has that ever worked?

LET'S KILL HITLER

'Bullets and bombs aren't the answer to everything.'

THE DOCTOR, *THE SEEDS OF DOOM*

'Weapons. Always useless in the end.'

THE DOCTOR, *REMEMBRANCE OF THE DALEKS*

'Pacifism only works when everybody feels the same.'

IAN, *THE DALEKS*

'I don't think that right is on anyone's side in war, Miss Hardaker.'

REVEREND WAINWRIGHT, *THE CURSE OF FENRIC*

'When you get back to Skaro, you'll all be national heroes. Everybody will want to hear about your adventures... So be careful how you tell that story, will you? Don't glamourise it. Don't make war sound like an exciting and thrilling game... Tell them about the members of your mission that will not be returning... Tell them about the fear, otherwise your people might relish the idea of war. We don't want that.'

THE DOCTOR, *PLANET OF THE DALEKS*

ACE: It's a missile convoy.

THE DOCTOR: A *nuclear* missile convoy.

ACE: How do you know?

THE DOCTOR: It has a graveyard stench.

BATTLEFIELD

'All over the world, fools are poised ready to let death fly. Machines of death, Morgaine, are screaming from above. A light, brighter than the sun. Not a war between armies nor a war between nations, but just death. Death gone mad. A child looks up at the sky, his eyes turn to cinders. No more tears, only ashes. Is this honour? Is this war? Are these the weapons you would use? Tell me!'

THE DOCTOR, *BATTLEFIELD*

IZLYR: We reject violence, except in self-defence.

JO: What about Ssorg's gun? This is supposed to be a peaceful mission.

IZLYR: Unfortunately, in order to preserve peace, it is necessary to survive.

THE CURSE OF PELADON

THE MILITARY

THE DOCTOR: Well quite frankly, Brigadier, I fail to see the value of a lot of idiot soldiers clumping about the place.

THE BRIGADIER: Oh, you've been thankful enough sometimes, Doctor.

THE GREEN DEATH

'I sometimes think that military intelligence is a contradiction in terms.'

THE DOCTOR, *TERROR OF THE AUTONS*

THE DOCTOR: Hello. Who are you?

RESTAC: Restac, Military commander.

THE DOCTOR: Oh dear, really? There's always a military, isn't there?

COLD BLOOD

THE DOCTOR: Never cared much for the word impregnable. Sounds a bit too much like unsinkable.

HARRY: What's wrong with unsinkable?

THE DOCTOR: Nothing, as the iceberg said to the *Titanic*... Glug, glug, glug...

ROBOT

'That's typical of the military mind, isn't it? Present them with a new problem, and they start shooting at it.'

THE DOCTOR, *DOCTOR WHO AND THE SILURIANS*

'Among all the varied wonders of the universe there's nothing so firmly clamped shut as the military mind.'

THE DOCTOR, *BATTLEFIELD*

'The military mind at its most scintillating. Faced with a problem they blast it off the face of the Earth.'

THE DOCTOR, *TERROR OF THE AUTONS*

'Chap with the wings there. Five rounds rapid.'

THE BRIGADIER, *THE DAEMONS*

THE TIME WAR

'The Time War. The whole universe convulsed. The Time War raged. Invisible to smaller species but devastating to higher forms.'

THE GELTH, *THE UNQUIET DEAD*

'Perhaps it's time. This is only the furthest edge of the Time War. But at its heart millions die every second. Lost in bloodlust and insanity. With Time itself resurrecting them to find new ways of dying, over and over again. A travesty of life.'

THE PARTISAN, *THE END OF TIME*

'I've had many faces, many lives. I don't admit to all of them. There's one life I've tried very hard to forget. He was the Doctor who fought in the Time War, and that was the day he did it. The day I did it. The day he killed them all. The last day of the Time War. The war to end all wars between my people and the Daleks. And in that battle there was a man with more blood on his hands than any other, a man who would commit a crime that would silence the universe. And that man was me.'

THE DOCTOR, *THE DAY OF THE DOCTOR*

'For a long time I thought I was just a survivor, but I'm not. I'm the winner. That's who I am. The Time Lord Victorious.'

THE DOCTOR, *THE WATERS OF MARS*

'Everything she did was so human. She brought you back to life but she couldn't control it. She brought you back for ever. That's something, I suppose. The final act of the Time War was life.'

THE DOCTOR, *UTOPIA*

DANGER

'Hello, I'm the Doctor! I believe you want to kill me.'

THE DOCTOR, *SILVER NEMESIS*

ROSE: Mauve?

THE DOCTOR: The universally recognised colour for danger.

ROSE: What happened to red?

THE DOCTOR: That's just humans. By everyone else's standards, red's camp. Oh, the misunderstandings. All those red alerts, all that dancing.'

THE EMPTY CHILD

'The situation, Lavel, is normal. It doesn't get much worse than that.'

THE BRIGADIER, *BATTLEFIELD*

'Arms. Legs. Neck. Head. Nose. I'm fine. Everyone else?'

THE DOCTOR, *MIDNIGHT*

THE DOCTOR: So much fuss over a little water.

PERI: No, but pink water...

THE DOCTOR: Are you frightened it might clash with what you're wearing?

PERI: No, I'm more concerned I might clash with what lives in it.

THE TRIAL OF A TIME LORD: MINDWARP

'Every time, it's rule one. Don't wander off. I tell them, I do. Rule one. There could be anything on this ship.'

THE DOCTOR, *THE GIRL IN THE FIREPLACE*

'A risk shared is a risk doubled.'

THE DOCTOR, *FRONTIOS*

TURLOUGH: We're running out of places to run.

TEGAN: It's the story of our lives.

THE AWAKENING

THE DOCTOR: We're up a gum tree without a paddle.

K-9: Define gum tree.

THE DOCTOR: Well, it's a tree that gives gum.

K-9: Explain use of paddle in gum tree.

THE DOCTOR: You wouldn't understand, K-9.

K-9: Affirmative.

THE HORNS OF NIMON

'We've found something. It looks like metal. Like some sort of seal. I've got a nasty feeling the word might be trapdoor. Not a good word, trapdoor. Never met a trapdoor I liked.'

THE DOCTOR, *THE IMPOSSIBLE PLANET*

'Don't wander off. Now, I'm not just saying don't wander off, I mean it. Otherwise you'll wander off and the next thing you know, somebody's going to have to start rescuing somebody.'

THE DOCTOR, *NIGHTMARE IN SILVER*

'Something's wrong... we haven't been attacked yet.'

THE DOCTOR, *BATTLEFIELD*

'Jamie, we're already in the lion's den. What we've got to concentrate on is keeping our heads out of his mouth.'

THE DOCTOR, *FURY FROM THE DEEP*

VIOLENCE

SEAN: You are so on the team. Next week we've got the Crown and Anchor. We're going to annihilate them.

THE DOCTOR: Annihilate? No. No violence, do you understand me? Not while I'm around. Not today, not ever. I'm the Doctor, the Oncoming Storm... and you basically meant beat them in a football match, didn't you?

SEAN: Yeah.

THE DOCTOR: Lovely. What sort of time?

THE LODGER

'Sad really, isn't it? People spend all their time making nice things, and other people come along and break them.'

THE DOCTOR, *THE ENEMY OF THE WORLD*

BROCK: His scarf killed Stimson!

THE DOCTOR: Arrest the scarf, then.

THE LEISURE HIVE

'Frightening, isn't it, to find there are others better versed in death than human beings.'

THE DOCTOR, *REMEMBRANCE OF THE DALEKS*

'Why can't people be nice to one another, just for a change? I mean, I'm an alien and you don't want to drag me into a swamp, do you? You do!'

THE DOCTOR, *FULL CIRCLE*

'There should have been another way.'

THE DOCTOR, *WARRIORS OF THE DEEP*

THE DOCTOR: When you find something brand new in the world, something you've never seen before, what's the next thing you look for?

STRAX: A grenade.

THE SNOWMEN

ROMANA: You should go into partnership with a glazier. You'd have a truly symbiotic working relationship.

DUGGAN: What?

ROMANA: I'm just pointing out that you break a lot of glass.

DUGGAN: You can't make an omelette without breaking eggs.

ROMANA: If you wanted an omelette, I'd expect to find a pile of broken crockery, a cooker in flames and an unconscious chef.

CITY OF DEATH

'Yes, that's your philosophy, isn't it? If it moves, hit it … If you do that one more time, Duggan, I'm going to take very, very severe measures … I'm going to ask you not to.'

THE DOCTOR, *CITY OF DEATH*

'Killing me isn't going to help you. It isn't going to do me much good either, is it?'

THE DOCTOR, *THE FACE OF EVIL*

'You know, I am so constantly outwitting the opposition, I tend to forget the delights and satisfaction of the gentle art of fisticuffs.'

THE DOCTOR, *THE ROMANS*

'If you're bleeding, look for a man with scars.'

LEELA, *THE ROBOTS OF DEATH*

'I strongly advise the issuing of scissor grenades, limbo vapour and triple blast brain splitters… Remember, we are going to the north.'

STRAX, *THE CRIMSON HORROR*

LITEFOOT: I think this entire enterprise is extremely rash and ill-considered.

THE DOCTOR: My dear Litefoot, I've got a lantern and a pair of waders, and possibly the most fearsome piece of hand artillery in all England. What could possibly go wrong?

LITEFOOT: Well, *that* for a start. It hasn't been fired for fifty years. If you try to use it, it'll probably explode in your face.

THE DOCTOR: Explode? Unthinkable. It was made in Birmingham.

THE TALONS OF WENG-CHIANG

'If there's one thing I can't stand, it's being tortured by someone with cold hands.'

THE DOCTOR, *CITY OF DEATH*

'Whereas yours is a simple case of sociopathy, Dibber, my malaise is much more complex. "A deep-rooted maladjustment", my psychiatrist said. "Brought on by an infantile inability to come to terms with the more pertinent, concrete aspects of life" … Mind you, I had just attempted to kill him.'

SABALOM GLITZ, *THE TRIAL OF A TIME LORD: THE MYSTERIOUS PLANET*

THE DOCTOR: Hello. I'm the Doctor.

VARNE: Unless you help us, you won't be for very much longer.

ATTACK OF THE CYBERMEN

'How is it wherever I go in the universe there are always people like you pointing guns or phasers or blasters?'

THE DOCTOR, *THE HORNS OF NIMON*

ROSE: Doctor, they've got guns.

THE DOCTOR: And I haven't. Which makes me the better person, don't you think? They can shoot me dead, but the moral high ground is mine.

ARMY OF GHOSTS

'That's what guns are for. Pull a trigger, end a life. Simple, isn't it… Why don't you do it, then? Look me in the eye, pull the trigger, end my life.'

THE DOCTOR, *THE HAPPINESS PATROL*

'Guns can seriously damage your health, you know!'

THE DOCTOR, *THE MARK OF THE RANI*

'Now drop your weapons, or I'll kill him with this deadly jelly baby.'

THE DOCTOR, *THE FACE OF EVIL*

NIMON: Silence. Later you will be questioned, tortured and killed.

THE DOCTOR: Well I hope you get it in the right order.

THE HORNS OF NIMON

THE INQUISITOR: I find primitive physical violence distressing.

THE DOCTOR: So do I, ma'am. Especially when I'm on the receiving end.

THE TRIAL OF A TIME LORD: THE MYSTERIOUS PLANET

STRAX: If she hasn't made contact by nightfall, I suggest a massive frontal assault on the factory, madam. Casualties can be kept to perhaps as little as eighty per cent.

VASTRA: I think there may be subtler ways of proceeding, Strax.

STRAX: Suit yourself.

THE CRIMSON HORROR

'I say, what a wonderful butler. He's so violent.'

THE DOCTOR, *CITY OF DEATH*

'You fought her off with a water pistol. I bloody love you!'

DONNA, *THE FIRES OF POMPEII*

TYRANNY

'Conquered the Earth? You poor, pathetic creatures. Don't you realise? Before you attempt to conquer the Earth, you will have to destroy all living matter.'

THE DOCTOR, *THE DALEK INVASION OF EARTH*

'There are only two sides today, Barbara. Those who rule by fear and treachery, and those who fight for reason and justice. Anyone who betrays these principles is worse than the devil in hell!'

JULES RENAN, *THE REIGN OF TERROR*

THE DOCTOR: I'll say one thing for you, Davros. Your conversation is totally predictable. You're like a deranged child, all this talk of killing, revenge and destruction.

DAVROS: It is the only path to ultimate power.

RESURRECTION OF THE DALEKS

'Krynoid on the outside, a madman lurking inside, not a happy situation.'

THE DOCTOR, *THE SEEDS OF DOOM*

'One man's law is another man's crime.'

THE DOCTOR, *THE EDGE OF DESTRUCTION*

'Bad laws were made to be broken.'

THE DOCTOR, *THE MACRA TERROR*

ROMANA: The Black Guardian's a real threat.

THE DOCTOR: Some galactic hobo with ideas above his station, the cosmos is full of them.

THE LEISURE HIVE

'This is all too easy. A great pity. These facile victories only leave me hungry for more conquest.'

THE MASTER, *CASTROVALVA*

'What is the one thing evil cannot face? Not ever? … Itself.'

THE DOCTOR, *KINDA*

'Intruders from other planets always say they wish to talk, but all they mean to do is destroy.'

SECOND SENSORITE, *THE SENSORITES*

'Doctor, I offer you power. Power to corrupt, to destroy. Think of the exhilaration of that power. Serve me and live.'

THE CELESTIAL TOYMAKER, *THE CELESTIAL TOYMAKER*

THE NUCLEUS: The age of man is over, Doctor. The age of the virus has begun.

THE DOCTOR: I've heard it all before. You megalomaniacs are all the same.

THE INVISIBLE ENEMY

'Revenge! Best served hot.'

THE MASTER, *LAST OF THE TIME LORDS*

THE DOCTOR: We have the power to do anything we like. Absolute power over every particle in the universe. Everything that has ever existed or ever will exist. As from this moment – are you listening to me, Romana? ... Because, if you're not listening, I can make you listen because I can do anything... As from this moment there's no such thing as free will in the entire universe. There's only my will, because I possess the Key to Time!

ROMANA: Doctor – are you all right?

THE DOCTOR: Well, of course I'm all right. But supposing I wasn't all right? Well, this thing makes me feel in such a way I'd be very worried if I felt like that about someone else feeling like this about that. Do you understand?

THE ARMAGEDDON FACTOR

A CARNIVAL OF MONSTERS

'Don't fire until you see the green of its tentacles.'

THE DOCTOR, *HORROR OF FANG ROCK*

ELLIOT: Have you met monsters before?

THE DOCTOR: Yeah.

ELLIOT: You scared of them?

THE DOCTOR: No, they're scared of me.

THE HUNGRY EARTH

LIZ: I deal with facts, not science fiction ideas.

THE BRIGADIER: Miss Shaw, I'm not a fool. I don't chase shadows. What you don't understand is that there might, there is a remote possibility that outside your cosy little world other things could exist.

SPEARHEAD FROM SPACE

'You know, just once I'd like to meet an alien menace that wasn't immune to bullets.'

THE BRIGADIER, *ROBOT*

ROMANA: Are there many creatures like that in other worlds?

THE DOCTOR: Millions. Millions! You shouldn't have volunteered if you are scared of a little thing like that.

THE RIBOS OPERATION

'Makes you wonder what could be so bad it doesn't actually mind us thinking it's a vampire.'

THE DOCTOR, *VAMPIRES OF VENICE*

THE DOCTOR: Any intelligent life form?

TARON: Oh, yes. The Spiridons. They're invisible.

THE DOCTOR: I'd very much like to see one of them.

PLANET OF THE DALEKS

IAN: Maybe we could talk to them, make them understand?

THE DOCTOR: Apart from rubbing our back legs together like some sort of grasshopper, I doubt if we could get on speaking terms with them.

THE WEB PLANET

'Well, I never thought I'd fire in anger at a dratted caterpillar...'

THE BRIGADIER, *THE GREEN DEATH*

COMMANDER: I don't understand. Why was it necessary for him to make himself look human?

THE DOCTOR: Well, if you'd seen a Usurian you'd know what I mean. They look like sea kale with eyes. I mean, would you take orders from a lump of seaweed?

THE SUN MAKERS

'When you've travelled as much as I have, you'll learn never to judge by appearances. These creatures may look like chickens, but for all we know, they're the intelligent life form on this planet.'

THE DOCTOR, *CARNIVAL OF MONSTERS*

BRIAN: Are those pterodactyls?

THE DOCTOR: Yes. On any other occasion, I'd be thrilled. Exposed on a beach, less thrilled.

DINOSAURS ON A SPACESHIP

THE DOCTOR: Excuse me, do you mind not farting while I'm saving the world?

JOSEPH GREEN: Would you rather silent but deadly?

ALIENS OF LONDON

THE DOCTOR: Somehow the Krynoid can channel its power to other plants. All the vegetation on this planet is about to turn hostile.

THACKERAY: You mean like aggressive rhubarb?

THE DOCTOR: Yes, aggressive rhubarb.

BERESFORD: What about homicidal gooseberries?

THE SEEDS OF DOOM

'You really can't go on calling yourself Morbius. There's very little of Morbius left. Why don't you think of another name? Potpourri would be appropriate.'

THE DOCTOR, *THE BRAIN OF MORBIUS*

'We're being attacked by statues in a crashed ship. There isn't a manual for this.'

THE DOCTOR, *FLESH AND STONE*

'As my dear mother always used to say – born under the sign of Patus, middle cusp, she was – if you can help anybody, like preventing them from being eaten by a monster, then do so. They might be grateful.'

ORGANON, *THE CREATURE FROM THE PIT*

RANQUIN: Kroll is all wise, all seeing—

THE DOCTOR: All baloney. Kroll couldn't tell the difference between you and me and a half an acre of dandelion and burdock.

THE POWER OF KROLL

THE DOCTOR: A Nestene is a ruthlessly aggressive intelligent alien life form.

JO: Well, what do they look like?

THE DOCTOR: Well I suspect myself their basic form is analogous to a cephalopod.

JO: What's a cephalopod?

THE DOCTOR: An octopus. I thought you took an A level in science.

JO: I didn't say I passed.

TERROR OF THE AUTONS

DALEKS

'Exterminate!'

THE DALEKS, VARIOUS

COMMANDER SHARREL: You know the Daleks?

THE DOCTOR: Oh, better than you could possibly imagine.

DESTINY OF THE DALEKS

'Advance and attack! Attack and destroy! Destroy and rejoice!'

THE DALEKS, *THE CHASE*

'Daleks are such boring conversationalists.'

THE DOCTOR, *REMEMBRANCE OF THE DALEKS*

'Inside each of those shells is a living, bubbling lump of hate.'

THE DOCTOR, *DEATH TO THE DALEKS*

'You are my enemy! And I am yours. You are everything I despise. The worst thing in all creation. I've defeated you – time and time again I've defeated you. I sent you back into the Void. I saved the whole of reality from you. I am the Doctor. And you are the Daleks.'

THE DOCTOR, *VICTORY OF THE DALEKS*

THE DOCTOR: I thought you'd run out of ways to make me sick ... You think hatred is beautiful.

DALEK PRIME MINISTER: Perhaps that is why we have never been able to kill you.

ASYLUM OF THE DALEKS

GILMORE: Doctor, my men have just put three high-explosive grenades into a confined area. Nothing even remotely human could have survived that.

THE DOCTOR: That's the point group, Group Captain, it isn't even remotely human.

REMEMBRANCE OF THE DALEKS

'If you're supposed to be the superior race of the universe, why don't you try climbing after us?'

THE DOCTOR, *DESTINY OF THE DALEKS*

ADAM: Great big alien death machine defeated by a flight of stairs …

DALEK: Elevate!

DALEK

DALEK: Have pity!

THE DOCTOR: Why should I? You never did.

DALEK

'Pity? I have no understanding of the word. It is not registered in my vocabulary bank. Exterminate.'

DALEK, *GENESIS OF THE DALEKS*

DALEKS: Save the Daleks! Save the Daleks!

THE DOCTOR: Well. This is new.

ASYLUM OF THE DALEKS

GILMORE: What am I dealing with? Little green men?

THE DOCTOR: No, little green blobs in bonded-polycarbide armour.

REMEMBRANCE OF THE DALEKS

'It's called a Dalek. And it's not just metal, it's alive … Inside that shell is a creature born to hate. Whose only thought is to destroy everything and everyone that isn't a Dalek too. It won't stop until it's killed every human being alive.'

THE DOCTOR, *DALEKS IN MANHATTAN*

'Never underestimate the Daleks.'

THE DOCTOR, *PLANET OF THE DALEKS*

'One Dalek is capable of exterminating all!'

DALEK, *THE DALEKS' MASTER PLAN*

'It can do many things … But the thing it does most efficiently is exterminate human beings. It destroys them, without mercy, without conscience. It destroys them. Utterly. Completely.'

THE DOCTOR, *THE POWER OF THE DALEKS*

'Today, the Kaled race is ended, consumed in a fire of war, but from its ashes will rise a new race, the supreme creature, the ultimate conqueror of the universe – the Dalek! The action you take today is the beginning of a journey that will take the Daleks to their destiny of universal and absolute supremacy.'

DAVROS, *GENESIS OF THE DALEKS*

'The moment that we forget that we're dealing with people, then we're no better off than the machines that we came here to destroy. When we start acting and thinking like the Daleks, Taron, the battle is lost.'

THE DOCTOR, *PLANET OF THE DALEKS*

'But if I kill, wipe out a whole intelligent life form, then I become like them. I'd be no better than the Daleks.'

THE DOCTOR, *GENESIS OF THE DALEKS*

'The Daleks will triumph. We cannot fail. The Daleks' true destiny is to rule the universe.'

SUPREME DALEK, *RESURRECTION OF THE DALEKS*

THE DOCTOR: The Daleks have failed! Why don't you finish the job and make the Daleks extinct. Rid the universe of your filth. Why don't you just die?

DALEK: You would make a good Dalek.

DALEK

'Sealed inside your casing. Not feeling anything, ever, from birth to death, locked inside a cold metal cage. Completely alone. That explains your voice. No wonder you scream.'

THE DOCTOR, *DOOMSDAY*

'You stupid tin boxes.'

THE MASTER, *FRONTIER IN SPACE*

DALEK JAST: Daleks are supreme. Humans are weak.

DALEK SEC: But there are millions of humans and only four of us. If we are supreme, why are we not victorious? The Cult of Skaro was created by the Emperor for this very purpose. To imagine new ways of survival.

DALEK THAY: But we must remain pure.

DALEK SEC: No, Dalek Thay. Our purity has brought us to extinction.

DALEKS IN MANHATTAN

THE DOCTOR: Dalek hunting is a terminal pastime.

ACE: So what are we doing?

THE DOCTOR: Dalek hunting.

REMEMBRANCE OF THE DALEKS

'We are entombed, but we live on. This is only the beginning. We will prepare. We will grow stronger. When the time is right, we will emerge and take our rightful place as the supreme power of the universe!'

DALEK, *GENESIS OF THE DALEKS*

'The trouble with Daleks is, they take so long to say anything. Probably die of boredom before they shoot me.'

THE DOCTOR, *THE TIME OF THE DOCTOR*

SUPREME DALEK: You are the Doctor. You must be exterminated.

THE DOCTOR: Don't mess with me, sweetheart.

VICTORY OF THE DALEKS

DALEK SEC: My Daleks, just understand this. If you choose death and destruction, then death and destruction will choose you.

DALEK THAY: Incorrect. We will always survive.

EVOLUTION OF THE DALEKS

'The Daleks are never defeated!'

SUPREME DALEK, *PLANET OF THE DALEKS*

'They survive. They always survive, while I lose everything.'

THE DOCTOR, *DALEKS IN MANHATTAN*

'Just touch these two strands together and the Daleks are finished. Have I that right? … You see, some things could be better with the Daleks. Many future worlds will become allies just because of their fear of the Daleks … Listen, if someone who knew the future pointed out a child to you and told you that that child would grow up totally evil, to be a ruthless dictator who would destroy millions of lives, could you then kill that child? … Do I have the right?'

THE DOCTOR, *GENESIS OF THE DALEKS*

CYBERMEN

KRAIL: Feelings? I do not understand that word.

THE DOCTOR: Emotions. Love, pride, hate, fear. Have you no emotions, sir?

THE TENTH PLANET

BENOIT: Have you no mercy?

CYBERMAN: It is unnecessary.

THE MOONBASE

CYBERLEADER: Daleks, be warned. You have declared war upon the Cybermen.

DALEK SEC: This is not war. This is pest control.

DOOMSDAY

'We think of the humans. We think of their difference and their pain. They suffer in the skin. They must be upgraded.'

CYBERMAN, *THE AGE OF STEEL*

CYBERMAN: You know our ways. You must be destroyed.

THE DOCTOR: Yes, well, I was afraid you'd get back to that.

THE WHEEL IN SPACE

'You've no home planet, no influence, nothing. You're just a pathetic bunch of tin soldiers skulking about the galaxy in an ancient spaceship.'

THE DOCTOR, *REVENGE OF THE CYBERMEN*

'Oh, Lumic, you're a clever man. I'd call you a genius, except I'm in the room. But everything you've invented, you did to fight your sickness. And that's brilliant. That is so human. But once you get rid of sickness and mortality, then what's there to strive for, eh? The Cybermen won't advance. You'll just stop. You'll stay like this for ever. A metal Earth with metal men and metal thoughts, lacking the one thing that makes this planet so alive. People. Ordinary, stupid, brilliant people.'

THE DOCTOR, *THE AGE OF STEEL*

'The trouble with Cybermen is they've got hydraulic muscles, and of course hydraulic brains to go with them.'

THE DOCTOR, *REVENGE OF THE CYBERMEN*

THE DOCTOR: That's a living brain jammed inside a cybernetic body, with a heart of steel. All emotions removed.

ROSE: Why no emotions?

THE DOCTOR: Because it hurts.

RISE OF THE CYBERMEN

'It's hard to fight an enemy that uses your armies as spare parts.'

PORRIDGE, *NIGHTMARE IN SILVER*

DALEK SEC: You are superior in only one respect.

CYBERLEADER: What is that?

DALEK SEC: You are better at dying.

DOOMSDAY

CYBERLEADER: If humans had not had the resources of Voga, the Cyber War would have ended in glorious triumph.

THE DOCTOR: It was a glorious triumph, for human ingenuity. They discovered your weakness and invented the glitter gun, and that was the end of Cybermen, except as gold-plated souvenirs that people use as hat stands.

REVENGE OF THE CYBERMEN

CYBERMAN: You are the Doctor.

THE DOCTOR: Correct. And the Doctor always gives you a choice. Deactivate yourself, or I deactivate you.

CLOSING TIME

SONTARANS

'That's a Sontaran spaceship, to be precise, and tremendously powerful for its size, just like its owner.'

THE DOCTOR, *THE TIME WARRIOR*

SARAH: You killed him!

STYRE: That is my function. I am a warrior.

THE SONTARAN EXPERIMENT

'Sontarans never do anything without a military reason.'

THE DOCTOR, *THE SONTARAN EXPERIMENT*

STOR: I am Commander Stor, of the Sontaran Special Space Service.

THE DOCTOR: The SSSS. Isn't that carrying alliteration a little far?

THE INVASION OF TIME

'You have a primary and secondary reproductive cycle. It is an inefficient system, you should change it.'

LINX, *THE TIME WARRIOR*

THE DOCTOR: Sontaran. Clone warrior race. Factory produced, whole legions at a time. Two genders is a bit further than he can count.

STRAX: Sir, do not discuss my reproductive cycle in front of enemy girls. It's embarrassing.

THE SNOWMEN

THE MASTER

'I am the Master, and you will obey me…'

THE MASTER, VARIOUS

'That's my best enemy. He likes to be known as the Master, don't you?'

THE DOCTOR, *THE FIVE DOCTORS*

THE MASTER: I like it when you use my name.

THE DOCTOR: You chose it. Psychiatrist's field day.

THE SOUND OF DRUMS

'We are an explosive combination. One day, one of us might blot the other one out.'

THE DOCTOR, *SURVIVAL*

'Doctor, you're my intellectual equal. Almost. I have so few worthy opponents. When they've gone, I always miss them.'

THE MASTER, *TERROR OF THE AUTONS*

'He's on his last life, fighting to survive. And the science has shown us over and over, in the fight for survival there are no rules.'

THE DOCTOR, *DOCTOR WHO* (TV MOVIE)

'Envy is the beginning of all true greatness.'

THE MASTER, *LOGOPOLIS*

'Life is wasted on the living!'

THE MASTER, *DOCTOR WHO* (TV MOVIE)

THE MASTER: I am the Master!

PERI: So what? I'm Perpugilliam Brown and I can shout just as loud as you can.

PLANET OF FIRE

'I'm indestructible. The whole universe knows that.'

THE MASTER, *THE MARK OF THE RANI*

'I had estates. Do you remember my father's land back home? Pastures of red grass stretching far across the slopes of Mount Perdition. We used to run across those fields all day. Calling up at the sky. Look at us now.'

THE MASTER, *THE END OF TIME*

THE MASTER: Who else is there strong enough to give these humans the leadership they need?

THE DOCTOR: I seem to remember somebody else speaking like that. What was the bounder's name? Hitler. Yes, that's right, Adolf Hitler. Or was it Genghis Khan?

THE DAEMONS

'The drumming. Can't you hear it? I thought it would stop, but it never does. Never ever stops. Inside my head, the drumming, Doctor. The constant drumming.'

THE MASTER, *THE SOUND OF DRUMS*

'I'd like to try and take the Doctor alive if possible. If not, I'll blast him out of space. Pity though… I don't know, rocket fire at long range… somehow it lacks that personal touch.'

THE MASTER, *FRONTIER IN SPACE*

'Where I cannot win by stealth, I shall destroy. That way I cannot fail to win.'

THE MASTER, *THE KING'S DEMONS*

THE MASTER: One must rule or serve. That is the basic law of life. Why do you hesitate? Surely it's not loyalty to the Time Lords, who exiled you on one insignificant planet?

THE DOCTOR: You'll never understand, will you? I want to see the universe, not rule it.

COLONY IN SPACE

THE MASTER: I know this is going to be hard to believe, Doctor, but for once I mean you no harm.

THE DOCTOR: Like Alice, I try to believe three impossible things before breakfast.

THE FIVE DOCTORS

'You're a genius. You're stone cold brilliant, you are. I swear, you really are. But you could be so much more. You could be beautiful. With a mind like that, we could travel the stars. It would be my honour. Cause you don't need to own the universe. Just see it. To have the privilege of seeing the whole of time and space. That's ownership enough.'

THE DOCTOR, *THE END OF TIME*

MEL: How utterly evil!

THE MASTER: Thank you.

THE TRIAL OF A TIME LORD: THE ULTIMATE FOE

HOW INSULTING!

'You're a clumsy, ham-fisted idiot.'

THE DOCTOR, *THE ARK IN SPACE*

'I admire bravery and loyalty, sir. You have both of these. But, unfortunately you haven't any brain at all. I hate fools.'

THE DOCTOR, *THE CRUSADE*

'You swede-bashing cretin.'

COLBY, *IMAGE OF THE FENDAHL*

CHORLEY: There's no sense in us losing our temper, Miss Travers. I'm sorry that my journalistic style doesn't appeal to you, but there are millions of people it does.

ANNE: Yes, the gutter press has a very large following.

THE WEB OF FEAR

'You've been down here so long that you're beginning to think like worms.'

DORTMUN, *THE DALEK INVASION OF EARTH*

'Stubborn old mule'

THE DOCTOR, *HORROR OF FANG ROCK*

'My dear boy, if they had to deal with a man of your talents, they need hardly fear, need they?'

THE DOCTOR, *THE DALEK INVASION OF EARTH*

'They're policemen. We all know they're solid, sterling fellows, but their buttons are the brightest thing about them, don't you agree?'

JAGO, *THE TALONS OF WENG-CHIANG*

'Don't listen to him. It's just the ravings of a demented space tramp.'

ADRASTA, *THE CREATURE FROM THE PIT*

'You weak fool. You craven-hearted spineless poltroon.'

THE MASTER, *THE DEADLY ASSASSIN*

THE DOCTOR: I don't like your tone, sir.

CUTLER: And I don't like your face, nor your hair.

THE TENTH PLANET

'Yes, Packer. Our clever Doctor has outwitted you. Oh, then, that wouldn't be too difficult, would it?'

TOBIAS VAUGHN, *THE INVASION*

'Oh, I do not fear the thunder, you superstitious, dark-dodging decadent!'

HECTOR, *THE MYTH MAKERS*

'You're nothing. Nothing but a mass of superheated junk with delusions of grandeur.'

THE DOCTOR, *UNDERWORLD*

'Do hurry up! A hamster with a blunt penknife would do it quicker!'

THE DOCTOR, *THE ANDROIDS OF TARA*

'You, smart? Krelper, the wind whistles through your ears.'

STOTZ, *THE CAVES OF ANDROZANI*

'Yes, well I'll tell you something that should be of vital interest to you, Professor… That you, sir, are a nitwit!'

THE DOCTOR, *INFERNO*

'For such a little woman your mouth is too big.'

VILLAR, *THE WAR GAMES*

'Yes, let me guess. My theories appal you, my heresies outrage you, I never answer letters, and you don't like my tie.'

THE DOCTOR, *GHOST LIGHT*

'All right. All right, I'll confess… I confess you're a bigger idiot than I thought you were.'

THE DOCTOR, *THE DEADLY ASSASSIN*

'You know, you're a classic example of the inverse ratio between the size of the mouth and the size of the brain.'

THE DOCTOR, *THE ROBOTS OF DEATH*

'If you'd only try and use the little intelligence you have…'

THE DOCTOR, *INFERNO*

'Mickey, you were born in the dark.'

THE DOCTOR, *WORLD WAR THREE*

ROSE: My mother's cooking.

THE DOCTOR: Good. Put her on a slow heat and let her simmer.

WORLD WAR THREE

'You're happy to believe in something that's invisible, but if it's staring you in the face, nope, can't see it. There's a scientific explanation for that. You're thick.'

THE DOCTOR, *WORLD WAR THREE*

'Child, if only you'd think as an adult sometimes.'

THE DOCTOR, *THE DALEKS*

'You craven-gutted factory fodder.'

MANDREL, *THE SUN MAKERS*

'You male chauvinist bilge bag.'

ACE, *DRAGONFIRE*

'I can't decide whether you're a rogue, a halfwit or both!

THE DOCTOR, *THE REIGN OF TERROR*

'Jamie, it's a brilliant idea! It's so simple only you could have thought of it.'

THE DOCTOR, *THE DOMINATORS*

'Don't get all chippy with me, Vera Duckworth. Pop your clogs on and go and feed whippets.'

DONNA, *TURN LEFT*

'You hag! You perfidious hag! You virago! You harpy!'

ADA, *THE CRIMSON HORROR*

'Before we start all that, I just want to say thank you. Thank you, one and all. You ugly, fat-faced bunch of wet, snivelling traitors.'

THE MASTER, *THE SOUND OF DRUMS*

'Harry Sullivan is an imbecile!'

THE DOCTOR, *REVENGE OF THE CYBERMEN*

Chapter Four:
The Universe

'Well, it takes all sorts
to make a galaxy.'

THE DOCTOR, *TERROR OF THE ZYGONS*

THE INFINITE
WONDER OF
THE UNIVERSE

'We're at the very beginning, the new start of a solar system. Outside, the atoms are rushing towards each other. Fusing, coagulating, until minute little collections of matter are created. And so the process goes on and on until dust is formed. Dust then becomes solid entity. A new birth, of a sun and its planets.'

THE DOCTOR, *THE EDGE OF DESTRUCTION*

'There's always something to look at if you open your eyes.'

THE DOCTOR, *KINDA*

'It seems to me there's so much more to the world than the average eye is allowed to see. I believe, if you look hard, there are more wonders in this universe than you could ever have dreamed of… It's colour. Colour that holds the key. I can hear the colours – listen to them. Every time I step outside, I feel nature is shouting at me – "Come on! – Come and get me! Come on, come on! Capture my mystery!"'

VINCENT VAN GOGH, *VINCENT AND THE DOCTOR*

IAN: Doctor, why do you always show the greatest interest in the least important things?

THE DOCTOR: The least important things sometimes, my dear boy, lead to the greatest discoveries.

THE SPACE MUSEUM

THE DOCTOR: Millions of planets, millions of galaxies, and we're on this one. Molto bene. Bellissimo, says Donna, born in Chiswick. All you've got is a life of work and sleep, and telly and rent and tax and takeaway dinners, all birthdays and Christmases and two weeks holiday a year, and then you end up here. Donna Noble, citizen of the Earth, standing on a different planet. How about that Donna? Donna?

DONNA: Sorry, you were saying?

PLANET OF THE OOD

LIGHT: Everything is changing. All in flux. Nothing remains the same.

THE DOCTOR: Even remains change. It's this planet. It can't help itself.

GHOST LIGHT

'It's a big universe. Everything happens somewhere. Call it a coincidence. Call it an idea echoing among the stars. Personally, I call it a brilliant idea for a Christmas trip.'

THE DOCTOR, *THE DOCTOR, THE WIDOW AND THE WARDROBE*

'Planets come and go, stars perish. Matter disperses, coalesces, reforms into other patterns, other worlds. Nothing can be eternal.'

THE DOCTOR, *THE TRIAL OF A TIME LORD: THE MYSTERIOUS PLANET*

ADRIC: All those stars… Do you know them all?

THE DOCTOR: Well, just the interesting ones.

THE KEEPER OF TRAKEN

'There's all sorts of realities around us, different dimensions, billions of parallel universes all stacked up against each other. The Void is the space in between, containing absolutely nothing. Imagine that. Nothing. No light, no dark, no up, no down, no life, no time. Without end. My people called it the Void. The Eternals call it the Howling. But some people call it Hell.'

THE DOCTOR, *ARMY OF GHOSTS*

KERENSKY: I know what I'm doing. I am the foremost authority on temporal theory in the whole world. …

THE DOCTOR: Well, that's a very small place when you consider the size of the universe.

CITY OF DEATH

'You dreamt of another sky. New sun, new air, new life. A whole universe teeming with life. Why stand still when there's all that life out there.'

THE DOCTOR, *VOYAGE OF THE DAMNED*

'All the elements in your body were forged many, many millions of years ago, in the heart of a faraway star that exploded and died. That explosion scattered those elements across the desolations of deep space. After so, so many millions of years, these elements came together to form new stars and new planets. And on and on it went. The elements came together and burst apart, forming shoes and ships and sealing wax, and cabbages and kings. Until, eventually, they came together to make you. You are unique in the universe.'

THE DOCTOR, *THE RINGS OF AKHATEN*

'Life in some form will always go on.'

THE DOCTOR, *THE MUTANTS*

VINCENT: Hold my hand, Doctor. Try to see what I see. We are so lucky we are still alive to see this beautiful world. Look at the sky. It's not dark and black and without character. The black is in fact deep blue. And over there, lighter blue. And blowing through the blueness and the blackness, the wind swirling through the air and then, shining, burning, bursting through, the stars. Can you see how they roar their light? Everywhere we look, the complex magic of nature blazes before our eyes.

THE DOCTOR: I've seen many things, my friend. But you're right. Nothing quite as wonderful as the things you see.

VINCENT AND THE DOCTOR

'That's two impossible things we've seen so far tonight. Don't you love it when that happens?'

THE DOCTOR, *THE LAZARUS EXPERIMENT*

THE INDOMITABLE HUMAN RACE

'Homo sapiens. What an inventive, invincible species. It's only a few million years since they crawled up out of the mud and learned to walk. Puny, defenceless bipeds. They survived flood, famine and plague. They survived cosmic wars and holocausts, and now here they are amongst the stars, waiting to begin a new life, ready to outsit eternity. They're indomitable. Indomitable!'

THE DOCTOR, *THE ARK IN SPACE*

'I love humans. Always seeing patterns in things that aren't there.'

THE DOCTOR, *DOCTOR WHO* (TV MOVIE)

'This day is ending. Humankind is weak. You shelter from the dark. And yet, you have built all this... My planet is gone, destroyed in a great war, yet versions of this city stand throughout history. The human race always continues.'

DALEK CAAN, *DALEKS IN MANHATTAN*

'It may be irrational of me, but human beings are quite my favourite species.'

THE DOCTOR, *THE ARK IN SPACE*

'... the great breakout ... When your forefathers went leapfrogging across the solar system on their way to the stars. Asteroid belt's probably teeming with them now. New frontiersmen, pioneers waiting to spread across the galaxy like a tidal wave. Or a disease.'

THE DOCTOR, *THE INVISIBLE ENEMY*

'But what I wanted to say is, you know, when you're a kid, they tell you it's all, grow up, get a job, get married, get a house, have a kid, and that's it. But the truth is, the world is so much stranger than that. It's so much darker, and so much madder. And so much better.'

ELTON, *LOVE & MONSTERS*

'Consider the human species. They send hordes of settlers across space to breed, multiply, conquer and dominate. We have as much right to conquer you as you have to strike out across the stars.'

THE NUCLEUS, *THE INVISIBLE ENEMY*

'Funny little human brains. How do you get around in those things?'

THE DOCTOR, *THE DOCTOR DANCES*

'I'm a human being. Maybe not the stuff of legend but every bit as important as Time Lords, thank you.'

DONNA, *THE STOLEN EARTH*

'Don't you see, though? The ripe old smell of humans. You survived. Oh, you might have spent a million years evolving into clouds of gas, and another million as downloads, but you always revert to the same basic shape. The fundamental humans.'

THE DOCTOR, *UTOPIA*

'The nature of man, even in this day and age, hasn't altered at all. You still fear the unknown, like everyone else before you.'

STEVEN, *THE ARK*

'The human race makes sense out of chaos. Marking it out with weddings and Christmas and calendars. This whole process is beautiful, but only if it's being observed.'

THE DOCTOR, *THE RUNAWAY BRIDE*

THE DOCTOR: You know, I'll never understand the people of Earth. I have spent the day using, abusing, even trying to kill you. If you'd have behaved as I have, I should have been pleased at your demise.

PERI: It's called compassion, Doctor. It's the difference that remains between us.

THE TWIN DILEMMA

'Observe humanity. For all their faults they have such courage.'

DALEK SEC, *EVOLUTION OF THE DALEKS*

THE DARK SIDE OF HUMANITY

'Human race, greatest monsters of them all.'

THE MASTER, *LAST OF THE TIME LORDS*

VICTORIA: We've landed in a world of mad men.

THE DOCTOR: They're human beings, if that's what you mean, indulging their favourite past time. Trying to destroy each other.

THE ENEMY OF THE WORLD

'Some of my best friends are humans. When they get together in great numbers, other life forms sometimes suffer.'

THE DOCTOR, *THE INVISIBLE ENEMY*

'These Earth creatures are working to destroy the Sensorite nation. Their pleasant smile conceals sharp teeth, their soft words hide deadly threats.'

THE ADMINISTRATOR, *THE SENSORITES*

MOTHER OF MINE: He didn't just make himself human. He made himself an idiot.

SON OF MINE: Same thing, isn't it?

THE FAMILY OF BLOOD

'Your ancestors have a talent for self-destruction that borders on genius.'

THE DOCTOR, *IMAGE OF THE FENDAHL*

'Your species has the most amazing capacity for self-deception, matched only by its ingenuity when trying to destroy itself.'

THE DOCTOR, *REMEMBRANCE OF THE DALEKS*

'I gave them the wrong warning. I should've told them to run as fast as they can, run and hide because the monsters are coming. The human race.'

THE DOCTOR, *THE CHRISTMAS INVASION*

DALEK SEC: I feel... everything we wanted from mankind. Which is ambition, hatred, aggression. And war. Such a genius for war.

THE DOCTOR: No. That's not what humanity means.

DALEK SEC: I think it does. At heart this species is so very Dalek.

EVOLUTION OF THE DALEKS

DUGGAN: You're mad. You're insane. You're inhuman!

SCARLIONI: Quite so. When I compare my race to yours, human, I take the word inhuman as a great compliment.

CITY OF DEATH

AMBROSE: You could've let those things shoot me. You saved me.

THE DOCTOR: An eye for an eye. It's never the way. Now you show your son how wrong you were, how there's another way. You make him the best of humanity, in the way you couldn't be.

COLD BLOOD

SARAH: Don't you think that people have a right to choose what kind of life they want?

RUTH: People on Earth were allowed to choose. And see what kind of a world they made. Moral degradation, permissiveness, usury, cheating, lying, cruelty.

SARAH: There's also a lot of love and kindness and honesty. You've got a warped view of things.

INVASION OF THE DINOSAURS

EARTH

'I have a place in mind that's on the way, well, more or less, give or take a parsec or two. It's my home from home. It's called Earth.'

THE DOCTOR, *LOGOPOLIS*

ATRAXI: You are not of this world.

THE DOCTOR: No, but I've put a lot of work into it.

THE ELEVENTH HOUR

THE DOCTOR: And where are the Census Bureau going to send you next?

TREVOR: Earth. Have you been there?

THE DOCTOR: Once or twice.

TREVOR: Miserable sort of place.

THE DOCTOR: You're making me feel nostalgic.

THE HAPPINESS PATROL

ROMANA: Earth?!

THE DOCTOR: Well, I thought you'd be pleased!

ROMANA: I might have guessed. Your favourite planet.

THE DOCTOR: How do you know that?

ROMANA: Oh, everybody knows that.

THE STONES OF BLOOD

LIGHT: Earth. Why mention that wretched planet to me …
I once spent centuries faithfully cataloguing all the species
there, every organism from the smallest bacteria to the
largest ichthyosaur. But no sooner had I finished than it all
started changing. New species, new sub-species, evolution
running amok. I had to start amending my entries. Oh, the
task is endless.

THE DOCTOR: That's life.

GHOST LIGHT

SARAH: At least we're on Earth. I mean, just taste that air. I
love that fresh smell just after a rain shower.

THE DOCTOR: Yes, it does have that peculiar Earthy smell.

THE ANDROID INVASION

THE HUMAN CONDITION

THE DOCTOR: I'd have to settle down. Get a house or something. A proper house with… with doors and things. Carpets. Me, living in a house. Now that, that is terrifying.

ROSE: You'd have to get a mortgage.

THE DOCTOR: No.

ROSE: Oh, yes.

THE DOCTOR: I'm dying. That's it. I'm dying. It is all over.

THE IMPOSSIBLE PLANET

'I want to sit in a pub and drink a pint of beer again. I want to walk in a park and watch a cricket match. Above all, I want to belong somewhere, do something, instead of this aimless drifting around in space.'

IAN, *THE CHASE*

'If you're going to sit there wallowing in self-pity, I'll bite your nose.'

THE DOCTOR, *THE BRAIN OF MORBIUS*

'Everyone's scared when they're little. I used to be terrified of getting lost. Used to have nightmares about it. And then I got lost. Blackpool beach, bank holiday Monday, about ten billion people. I was about six. My worst nightmare come true… The world ended. My heart broke. And then my mum found me. We had fish and chips, and she drove me home and she tucked me up and she told me a story.'

CLARA, *THE RINGS OF AKHATEN*

BOSS: I will not be angered. I will eradicate anger. It affects efficiency.

THE DOCTOR: Nonsense. Sometimes it helps, you know.

THE GREEN DEATH

'I worked as a waitress in a fast food café. Day in, day out, same boring routine. Same boring life. It was all wrong. It didn't feel like me that was doing it at all. I felt like I'd fallen from another planet and landed in this strange girl's body, but it wasn't me at all. I was meant to be somewhere else. Each night I'd walk home and I'd look up at the stars through the gaps in the clouds, and I tried to imagine where I really came from. I dreamed that one day everything would come right. I'd be carried off back home, back to my real mum and dad. Then it actually happened and I ended up here. Ended up working as a waitress again, only this time I couldn't dream about going nowhere else. There wasn't nowhere else to go.'

ACE, *DRAGONFIRE*

'Oh, come on. Don't be upset. Yes, you failed. You failed, but congratulations – failure's one of the basic freedoms.'

THE DOCTOR, *THE ROBOTS OF DEATH*

'I was born on that planet. And so was my mum and so was my dad. And that makes me officially the last human being in this room. Cause you're not human. You've had it all nipped and tucked and flattened till there's nothing left. Anything human got chucked in the bin. You're just skin, Cassandra. Lipstick and skin.'

ROSE, *THE END OF THE WORLD*

GALLIFREY AND THE TIME LORDS

'The sky's a burnt orange, with the Citadel enclosed in a mighty glass dome, shining under the twin suns. Beyond that, the mountains go on for ever. Slopes of deep red grass, capped with snow.'

THE DOCTOR, *GRIDLOCK*

'A man is the sum of his memories, you know. A Time Lord even more so.'

THE DOCTOR, *THE FIVE DOCTORS*

THE DOCTOR: You can't fight Time Lords, Romana.

ROMANA: You did once.

THE DOCTOR: Hmm. And lost.

FULL CIRCLE

'Oh, you should have seen it, that old planet. The second sun would rise in the south, and the mountains would shine. The leaves on the trees were silver and, when they caught the light every morning, it looked like a forest on fire. When the autumn came, the breeze would blow through the branches like a song.'

THE DOCTOR, *GRIDLOCK*

'They used to call it the Shining World of the Seven Systems. And on the Continent of Wild Endeavour, in the Mountains of Solace and Solitude, there stood the Citadel of the Time Lords, the oldest and most mighty race in the universe, looking down on the galaxies below. Sworn never to interfere, only to watch. Children of Gallifrey, taken from their families at the age of eight to enter the Academy. Some say that's when it all began. When he was a child. That's when the Master saw eternity. As a novice, he was taken for initiation. He stood in front of the Untempered Schism. It's a gap in the fabric of reality through which could be seen the whole of the Vortex. You stand there, eight years old, staring at the raw power of time and space, just a child. Some would be inspired, some would run away, and some would go mad.'

THE DOCTOR, *THE SOUND OF DRUMS*

'And what of the Time Lords? I always thought of you as such a pompous race. Ancient, dusty senators, so frightened of change and chaos. And of course, they're all but extinct. Only you. The last.'

MR FINCH, *SCHOOL REUNION*

IAN: You're treating us like children.

THE DOCTOR: Am I? The children of my civilisation would be insulted.

AN UNEARTHLY CHILD

'Because that's how I see the universe. Every waking second I can see what is, what was, what could be, what must not. That's the burden of the Time Lords, Donna. And I'm the only one left.'

THE DOCTOR, *THE FIRES OF POMPEII*

'In all my travellings throughout the universe, I have battled against evil, against power-mad conspirators. I should have stayed here. The oldest civilisation – decadent, degenerate and rotten to the core. Power-mad conspirators? Daleks, Sontarans… Cybermen! They're still in the nursery compared to us. Ten million years of absolute power, that's what it takes to be really corrupt!'

THE DOCTOR, *THE TRIAL OF A TIME LORD: THE ULTIMATE FOE*

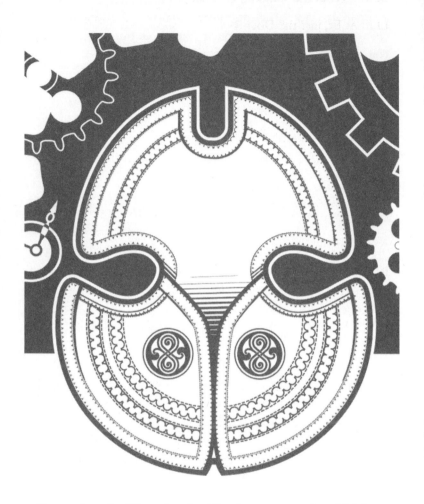

'Smart bunch, Time Lords. No dress sense, dreadful hats, but smart.'

THE DOCTOR, *JOURNEY TO THE CENTRE OF THE TARDIS*

RECEPTION NURSE: Patient's name?

LEELA: Er, just the Doctor.

RECEPTION NURSE: Place of origin?

LEELA: Gallifrey.

RECEPTION NURSE: Ireland?

LEELA: Oh, I expect so.

THE INVISIBLE ENEMY

JOAN: Ever the artist. Where did you learn to draw?

JOHN SMITH: Gallifrey.

JOAN: Is that in Ireland?

JOHN SMITH: Yes, it must be, yes.

JOAN: But you're not Irish?

HUMAN NATURE

INTERN: Tell me, where did you qualify, if I may ask?

THE DOCTOR: A place called Gallifrey.

INTERN: Gallifrey? No, I've not heard of it. Perhaps it's in Ireland.

THE DOCTOR: Probably.

THE HAND OF FEAR

THE DOCTOR: Oh, you shouldn't be worried. Time Lords have 90 lives.

ROMANA: How many have you got through, then?

THE DOCTOR: About a hundred and thirty.

THE CREATURE FROM THE PIT

REGENERATION

'That's the trouble with regeneration. You never quite know what you're going to get.'

THE DOCTOR, *CASTROVALVA*

ROSE: Can you change back?

THE DOCTOR: Do you want me to?

ROSE: Yeah.

THE DOCTOR: Oh.

ROSE: Can you?

THE DOCTOR: No.

BORN AGAIN

'Time Lords have this little trick, it's sort of a way of cheating death. Except it means I'm going to change, and I'm not going to see you again. Not like this. Not with this daft old face.'

THE DOCTOR, *THE PARTING OF THE WAYS*

'The old man must die and the new man will discover to his inexpressible joy that he has never existed.'

CHO-JE, *PLANET OF THE SPIDERS*

'New mouth. New rules. It's like eating after cleaning your teeth. Everything tastes wrong.'

THE DOCTOR, *THE ELEVENTH HOUR*

'I can still die. If I'm killed before regeneration then I'm dead. Even then. Even if I change, it feels like dying. Everything I am dies. Some new man goes sauntering away. And I'm dead.'

THE DOCTOR, *THE END OF TIME*

OTHER WORLDS

'If you could touch the alien sand and hear the cries of strange birds and watch them wheel in another sky, would that satisfy you?'

THE DOCTOR, *AN UNEARTHLY CHILD*

ROSE: If you are an alien, how comes you sound like you're from the North?

THE DOCTOR: Lots of planets have a north.

ROSE

'I have heard Davros say there is no intelligent life on other planets, so either he is wrong or you are lying.'

NYDER, *GENESIS OF THE DALEKS*

ANN: Then where are you from?

NYSSA: Traken.

ANN: Where's that?

SIR ROBERT: Near Esher, isn't it?

BLACK ORCHID

CHARLES: Now then, I'd better attend to that young man. What was his name again?

THE DOCTOR: Adric.

CHARLES: Scandinavian?

THE DOCTOR: Er, not quite. He's Alzarian.

CHARLES: I never could remember all those funny Baltic bits.

BLACK ORCHID

THE DOCTOR: 'If the thraskin puts his fingers in his ears, it is polite to shout.' That's an old Venusian proverb.

JO: What's a thraskin?

THE DOCTOR: Thraskin? Oh, it's an archaic word, seldom used since the twenty-fifth dynasty. The modern equivalent is plinge.

JO: What does plinge mean?

THE DOCTOR: Oh, for heaven's sake, Jo, I've just told you. It means thraskin.

JO: Oh, of course.

THE TIME MONSTER

THE DOCTOR: Florana. Probably one of the most beautiful planets in the universe.

SARAH: Well, count me out.

THE DOCTOR: It's always carpeted with perfumed flowers.

SARAH: I'm not listening.

THE DOCTOR: And its seas are as warm milk and the sands as soft as swan's down.

SARAH: No, Doctor.

THE DOCTOR: The streams flow with water that are clearer than the clearest crystal.

SARAH: No.

INVASION OF THE DINOSAURS

YRCANOS: On my planet of Krontep, a warrior queen fights alongside her king.

PERI: We're not on your planet.

YRCANOS: It doesn't matter. The rule still applies.

THE TRIAL OF A TIME LORD: MINDWARP

RORY: Got any more honeymoon ideas?

THE DOCTOR: Well, there's a moon that's made of actual honey. Well, not actual honey, and it's not actually a moon, and technically it's alive, and a bit carnivorous, but there are some lovely views.

A CHRISTMAS CAROL

'Have you ever looked up at the sky at night and seen those little lights? ... They are not ice crystals ... I believe they are suns, just like our own sun. And perhaps each sun has other worlds of its own, just as Ribos is a world.'

BINRO, *THE RIBOS OPERATION*

'There are worlds out there where the sky is burning, where the sea's asleep, and the rivers dream. People made of smoke, and cities made of song. Somewhere there's danger, somewhere there's injustice, and somewhere else the tea's getting cold. Come on, Ace, we've got work to do!'

THE DOCTOR, *SURVIVAL*

'No, Amy, it's definitely not the fifth moon of Cindie Colesta. I think I can see a Ryman's.'

THE DOCTOR, *THE LODGER*

AND WHEN YOU'RE HAVING A BAD DAY...

'Over a thousand years of saving the universe, Strax, you know the one thing I learned? The universe doesn't care.'

THE DOCTOR, *THE SNOWMEN*

Chapter Five:
The Journey

'Allons-y!'

THE DOCTOR

THE TARDIS

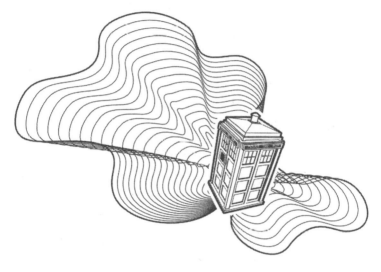

'Let me get this straight. A thing that looks like a police box, standing in a junkyard... it can move anywhere in time and space?'

IAN, *AN UNEARTHLY CHILD*

'Sorry, but you're about to make a very big mistake. Don't steal that one, steal this one. The navigation system's knackered, but you'll have much more fun.'

CLARA, *THE NAME OF THE DOCTOR*

IDRIS: Do you ever wonder why I chose you all those years ago?

THE DOCTOR: I chose you. You were unlocked.

IDRIS: Of course I was. I wanted to see the universe, so I stole a Time Lord and I ran away. And you were the only one mad enough.

THE DOCTOR'S WIFE

IAN: Ship?

THE DOCTOR: Yes, yes, ship. This doesn't roll along on wheels, you know.

AN UNEARTHLY CHILD

'It's my home. At least, it has been for a considerable number of years.'

THE DOCTOR, *THE TOMB OF THE CYBERMEN*

'But I need my ship. It's all I've got. Literally the only thing.'

THE DOCTOR, *THE IMPOSSIBLE PLANET*

IDRIS: You stole me. And I stole you.

THE DOCTOR: I borrowed you.

IDRIS: Borrowing implies the intention to return the thing that was taken. What makes you think I would ever give you back?

THE DOCTOR'S WIFE

THE DOCTOR: We're outside time. Of course, it always seems to take a long time but that depends upon the mood, I suppose.

JO: What, your mood?

THE DOCTOR: No, no, no, hers. No, the TARDIS's.

JO: You talk as if she was alive.

THE DOCTOR: It depends what you mean by alive, doesn't it?

THE TIME MONSTER

'The Type 40 capsule wasn't on the main syllabus, you see… Veteran and vintage vehicles was an optional extra.'

ROMANA, *THE PIRATE PLANET*

'When the TARDIS is on manual, you can't be certain of anything… It's harder to fly than you think. I mean, you don't just flick a switch.'

THE DOCTOR, *CASTROVALVA*

GREG: Well, I thought it'd be a bit more impressive than that.

THE DOCTOR: What did you expect? Some kind of space rocket with Batman at the controls?

INFERNO

RIVER: It's not supposed to make that noise. You leave the brakes on.

THE DOCTOR: Yeah, well, it's a brilliant noise. I love that noise.

THE TIME OF ANGELS

'Now then, you lot. Sarah, hold that down. Mickey, you hold that. Because you know why this TARDIS is always rattling about the place? Rose? That, there. It's designed to have six pilots, and I have to do it single-handed. Martha, keep that level. But not any more. Jack, there you go. Steady that. Now we can fly this thing. No, Jackie. No, no. Not you. Don't touch anything. Just stand back. Like it's meant to be flown. We've got the Torchwood Rift looped around the TARDIS by Mr Smith, and we're going to fly planet Earth back home. Right then. Off we go.'

THE DOCTOR, *JOURNEY'S END*

THE DOCTOR: The parametric engines are jammed. Orthogonal vector's gone. I'm almost out of ideas.

AVERY: Almost?

THE DOCTOR: Well, we could try stroking her and singing her a song.

AVERY: Will that help?

THE DOCTOR: Hard to say. Never has before.

THE CURSE OF THE BLACK SPOT

'This machine is a load of obsolete rubbish.'

STOR, *THE INVASION OF TIME*

STAPLEY: Is that how you travel, Doctor?

THE DOCTOR: Not exactly the first-class end of the market, but a serviceable vehicle, Captain.

TIME-FLIGHT

ANNE: It flies? Through time and space?

VICTORIA: Not exactly flies. Well, it's difficult to explain.

ANNE: Not half as difficult as it is to believe.

THE WEB OF FEAR

TODD: You don't actually go into space in that?

THE DOCTOR: Oh no. That would be completely impossible, wouldn't it?

TODD: Unlikely, anyway.

THE DOCTOR: If not ridiculous.

KINDA

THE DOCTOR: What nobody understands is, the advantage of my antiquated TARDIS is that it's fully equipped and completely reliable.

LEELA: Completely?

THE DOCTOR: Yes, well, almost completely.

THE INVASION OF TIME

BARBARA: Doctor, the trembling's stopped.

THE DOCTOR: Oh, my dear, I'm so glad you're feeling better.

BARBARA: No, not me, the ship.

THE RESCUE

TURLOUGH: Time will tell.

THE DOCTOR: Yes, indeed. Aboard the TARDIS it always does.

WARRIORS OF THE DEEP

'When a TARDIS is dying, sometimes the dimension dams start breaking down. They used to call it a size leak. All the bigger on the inside starts leaking to the outside. It grows. When I say that's the TARDIS, I don't mean it looks like the TARDIS, I mean it actually is the TARDIS. My TARDIS from the future. What else would they bury me in?'

THE DOCTOR, *THE NAME OF THE DOCTOR*

THE DOCTOR: You didn't always take me where I wanted to go.

IDRIS: No, but I always took you where you needed to go.

THE DOCTOR'S WIFE

IT'S A POLICE BOX...

IAN: It's a police box! What on earth's it doing here? These things are usually on the street. Look, feel it. Feel it. Do you feel it?

BARBARA: It's a faint vibration.

IAN: It's alive!

AN UNEARTHLY CHILD

JO: What on earth is he doing inside a horsebox?

THE DOCTOR: It isn't exactly a horsebox. It just happens to look like one.

JO: You mean there isn't a horse inside.

THE DOCTOR: No more than there's a policeman inside my police box.

TERROR OF THE AUTONS

LANE: It's a ship.

PACKARD: What, for midgets?

LANE: Or a coffin for a very large man.

WARRIORS' GATE

THE DOCTOR: I always read the instructions.

IDRIS: There's a sign on my front door. You have been walking past it for seven hundred years. What does it say?

THE DOCTOR: That's not instructions.

IDRIS: There's an instruction at the bottom. What does it say?

THE DOCTOR: Pull to open.

IDRIS: Yes. And what do you do?

THE DOCTOR: I push.

IDRIS: Every single time. Seven hundred years. Police box doors open out that way.

THE DOCTOR'S WIFE

ANDREWS: Are you responsible for this box, sir?

THE DOCTOR: Well, I try to be.

TIME-FLIGHT

BIGGER ON THE INSIDE

'I like the bit when someone says it's bigger on the inside. I always look forward to that.'

THE DOCTOR, *VAMPIRES OF VENICE*

'So we're in a box that's bigger on the inside, and it travels through time and space... How long have Scotland Yard had this?'

CANTON, *THE IMPOSSIBLE ASTRONAUT*

THE BRIGADIER: So this is what you've been doing with UNIT funds and equipment all this time. How's it done? Some sort of optical illusion?

THE DOCTOR : Oh, no, no, no. They come like this. Really.

THE THREE DOCTORS

AMY: I started to think that maybe you were just like a madman with a box.

THE DOCTOR: Amy Pond, there's something you'd better understand about me, because it's important, and one day your life may depend on it. I am definitely a madman with a box.

THE ELEVENTH HOUR

MARTHA: It's wood. It's like a box with that room just rammed in. It's bigger on the inside.

THE DOCTOR: Is it? I hadn't noticed.

SMITH AND JONES

THE DOCTOR: What matters is, we can communicate. We have got big problems now. They have taken the blue box, haven't they? The angels have the phone box.

LARRY: 'The angels have the phone box.' That's my favourite, I've got it on a T-shirt.

BLINK

'Let me stop you there. Bigger on the inside. Don't mind, do you, if we just skip to the end of that moment? Oh, and sorry I lied, by the way, when I said yours was bigger. Kitchen that way. Choice of bathrooms there, there, there.'

THE DOCTOR, *THE CURSE OF THE BLACK SPOT*

THE DOCTOR: It's called the TARDIS. It can travel anywhere in time and space. And it's mine.

CLARA: But it's… Well, look at it, it's…

THE DOCTOR: Go on, say it. Most people do.

CLARA: It's smaller on the outside.

THE DOCTOR: OK, that is a first.

THE SNOWMEN

WELCOME ABOARD

THE DOCTOR: My dear, why don't you come with us, hmm?

VICKI: In that old box?

THE DOCTOR: We can travel anywhere and everywhere in that old box as you call it. Regardless of space and time.

VICKI: Then it is a time machine?

THE DOCTOR: And if you like adventure, my dear, I can promise you an abundance of it.

THE RESCUE

HARRY: Oh, come along now, Doctor. We're both reasonable men. Now, we both know that police boxes don't go careering around all over the place.

THE DOCTOR: Do we?

HARRY: Of course we do. The whole idea's absurd.

THE DOCTOR: Is it? You wouldn't like to step inside a moment? Just to demonstrate that it is all an illusion?

ROBOT

LEELA: Take me with you.

THE DOCTOR: Why?

LEELA: What? Well. You like me, don't you?

THE DOCTOR: Well, yes, I suppose I do like you. But then, I like lots of people but I can't go carting them around the universe with me. Goodbye.

THE FACE OF EVIL

THE DOCTOR: Ace, where do you think you're going?

ACE: Perivale.

THE DOCTOR: Ah yes, but by which route? The direct route with Glitz, or the scenic route? Well? Do you fancy a quick trip round the twelve galaxies and then back to Perivale in time for tea?

DRAGONFIRE

TIME TRAVEL

'So, all of time and space, everything that ever happened or ever will. Where do you want to start?'

THE DOCTOR, *THE ELEVENTH HOUR*

'Time is not the boss of me.'

THE DOCTOR, *THE TIME OF ANGELS*

'The thing is, Adam, time travel's like visiting Paris. You can't just read the guide book, you've got to throw yourself in. Eat the food, use the wrong verbs, get charged double and end up kissing complete strangers. Or is that just me?'

THE DOCTOR, *THE LONG GAME*

'Gosh, that takes me back. Or forward. That's the trouble with time travel: you can never remember.'

THE DOCTOR, *THE ANDROIDS OF TARA*

'I do flit about a bit, you know... I don't seem to be able to help myself. There I am, just walking along minding my own business and pop! I'm on a different planet or even a different time. But enough of my problems.'

THE DOCTOR, *CITY OF DEATH*

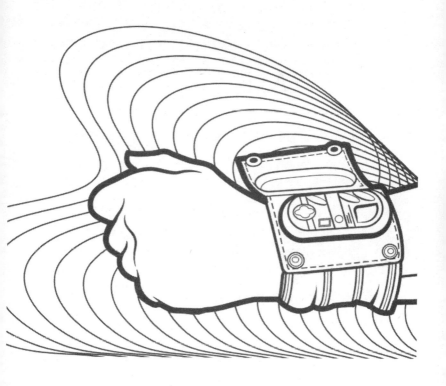

JACK: I used to be a Time Agent. It's called a Vortex manipulator. He's not the only one who can time travel.

THE DOCTOR: Oh, excuse me. That is not time travel. It's like, I've got a sports car and you've got a space hopper.

UTOPIA

'Vortex manipulator. Cheap and nasty time travel. Very bad for you. I'm trying to give it up.'

THE DOCTOR, *THE BIG BANG*

'Christmas. 1860. Happens once, just once and it's gone, it's finished, it'll never happen again. Except for you. You can go back and see days that are dead and gone a hundred thousand sunsets ago. No wonder you never stay still.'

ROSE, *THE UNQUIET DEAD*

'Lots of impossible things happen when you pass through time.'

THE DOCTOR, *THE WAR GAMES*

'You know, the thing about a time machine, though, you can run away all you like and still be home in time for tea, so what do you say? Anywhere. All of time and space, right outside those doors.'

THE DOCTOR, *THE BELLS OF SAINT JOHN*

THE DOCTOR: I also said this ship was generating enough power to punch a hole in the universe. I think we just found the hole. Must be a spatio-temporal hyperlink.

MICKEY: What's that?

THE DOCTOR: No idea. Just made it up. Didn't want to say magic door.

THE GIRL IN THE FIREPLACE

'It's always a big day tomorrow. We've got a time machine. I skip the little ones.'

THE DOCTOR, *THE BEAST BELOW*

'I mean, one minute you're in 1974 looking for ghosts, but all you have to do is open your eyes and talk to whoever's standing there. To you, I haven't been born yet, and to you I've been dead one hundred billion years. Is my body out there somewhere, in the ground?'

CLARA, *HIDE*

'Time travel is damage. It's like a tear in the fabric of reality. That is the scar tissue of my journey through the universe. My path through time and space from Gallifrey to Trenzalore.'

THE DOCTOR, *THE NAME OF THE DOCTOR*

'First things first? … But not necessarily in that order.'

THE DOCTOR, *MEGLOS*

TRAVEL BROADENS THE MIND

'Isn't it a better thing to travel hopefully than arrive?'

SUSAN, *THE SENSORITES*

'That's why I keep travelling. To be proved wrong.'

THE DOCTOR, *THE SATAN PIT*

'My dear girl, if I stopped to question the wisdom of my actions, I'd never have left Gallifrey.'

THE DOCTOR, *THE TRIAL OF A TIME LORD: MINDWARP*

CRAIG: I'm not much of a traveller.

THE DOCTOR: I can tell from your sofa.

CRAIG: My sofa?

THE DOCTOR: You're starting to look like it.

THE LODGER

ROMANA: Shall we take the lift or fly?

THE DOCTOR: Let's not be ostentatious.

ROMANA: All right. Let's fly, then.

THE DOCTOR: That would look silly. We'll take the lift.

CITY OF DEATH

'It's like I had that one day with you, and I was going to change. I was going to do so much. Then I woke up the next morning, same old life. It's like you were never there. And I tried. I did try. I went to Egypt. I was going to go barefoot and everything. And then it's all bus trips and guidebooks and don't drink the water, and two weeks later you're back home. It's nothing like being with you.'

DONNA, *PARTNERS IN CRIME*

ASTRID: So you travel alone?

THE DOCTOR: All the time. Just for fun. Well. That's the plan. Never quite works.

VOYAGE OF THE DAMNED

'You can't walk into the middle of a Western town and say you've come from outer space! Good gracious me. You would be arrested on a vagrancy charge!'

THE DOCTOR, *THE GUNFIGHTERS*

DONNA: I packed ages ago, just in case. Because I thought, hot weather, cold weather, no weather. He goes anywhere. I've gotta be prepared.

THE DOCTOR: You've got a hatbox.

DONNA: Planet of the Hats, I'm ready. I don't need injections, do I? You know, like when you go to Cambodia.

PARTNERS IN CRIME

'A straight line may be the shortest distance between two points, but it is by no means the most interesting.'

THE DOCTOR, *THE TIME WARRIOR*

'One day we'll know all the mysteries of the skies, and we'll stop our wandering.'

SUSAN, *MARCO POLO*

SUSAN: I never felt there was any time or place that I belonged to. I've never had any real identity.

DAVID: One day you will. There will come a time when you're forced to stop travelling, and you'll arrive somewhere.

THE DALEK INVASION OF EARTH

GETTING LOST

THE DOCTOR: We've come out of the time vortex at the wrong point, that's all. A few years too late.

SARAH: How many?

THE DOCTOR: Thirty thousand.

PLANET OF EVIL

THE DOCTOR: You're never without a sense of direction while there's an air flow. Air flows from A to B. Usually you want to be at B. Or at A.

TEGAN: I don't want to be at A or B, thank you very much.

FRONTIOS

'Oh, well, you weren't too far out, were you? Only about two hundred million miles.

BEN, *THE MOONBASE*

'Well, of course I can control it. Nine times out of ten. Well, seven times out of ten. Five times. Look. Never mind, let's see where we are.'

THE DOCTOR ON THE TARDIS, *THE ROBOTS OF DEATH*

THE DOCTOR: OK, so. Not London 1893. Yorkshire 1893. Near enough.

CLARA: You're making a habit of this, getting us lost.

THE DOCTOR: Sorry. It's much better than it used to be. Ooh, I once spent a hell of a long time trying to get a gobby Australian to Heathrow Airport.

THE CRIMSON HORROR

NYSSA: Where are we?

ADRIC: Earth again.

TEGAN: I did say I wanted to stay with the crew for a while. You can stop trying to get me back to Heathrow.

THE DOCTOR: I have.

TEGAN: You certainly know how to fly this crate, don't you?

BLACK ORCHID

JEFFERSON: You're telling me you don't know where you are?

THE DOCTOR: No idea. More fun that way.

THE IMPOSSIBLE PLANET

THE COLLECTOR: How did you get to Pluto?

LEELA: By accident, as usual.

THE SUN MAKERS

'Even I would find it hard to lose myself in a corridor.'

THE DOCTOR, *THE TRIAL OF A TIME LORD: THE MYSTERIOUS PLANET*

SARAH: We're lost.

THE DOCTOR: Mislaid, possibly.

SARAH: Oh, why don't we just go back to the TARDIS?

THE DOCTOR: For two good reasons. One, that I don't want to leave Peladon without having a word with my good friend, the King.

SARAH: Name dropper.

THE DOCTOR: And second.

SARAH: What?

THE DOCTOR: We *are* lost.

THE MONSTER OF PELADON

'Well, it's called a randomiser and it's fitted to the guidance system and operates under a very complex scientific principle called pot luck.'

THE DOCTOR, *THE ARMAGEDDON FACTOR*

'I always did have a terrible sense of direction. Still as long we keep going down.'

THE DOCTOR, *CASTROVALVA*

SPACECRAFT

'It's a spaceship. Brilliant! I got a spaceship on my first go.'

MICKEY, *THE GIRL IN THE FIREPLACE*

'Rocket. Blimey, a real proper rocket. Now that's what I call a spaceship. You've got a box, he's got a Ferrari. Come on, let's go see where he's going.'

DONNA, *PLANET OF THE OOD*

'Brilliant humans. Humans who travel all the way across space, flying in a tiny little rocket. Right into the orbit of a black hole, just for the sake of discovery. That's amazing! Do you hear me? Amazing, all of you.'

THE DOCTOR, *THE SATAN PIT*

'My dear man, I've spent more time in space than any astronaut on your staff. Not, I'll admit, in the rather primitive contraptions that you use, but I'll manage.'

THE DOCTOR, *THE AMBASSADORS OF DEATH*

THE MASTER: Well, that must be them. No other ship would be on a course for Earth at a time like this.

OGRON: We are on a course for Earth.

THE MASTER: Well naturally, because we're chasing them!

FRONTIER IN SPACE

THE DOCTOR: Uncle Josiah knows as much about its secrets as a hamburger knows about the Amazon desert.

ACE: Sounds a bit like you and the TARDIS.

GHOST LIGHT

'My ship's not made of tin like this old trash. Oh, good gracious me! Seems if I cough too loudly, the whole thing'd fall to pieces.'

THE DOCTOR, *GALAXY 4*

JAMIE: A spaceship? Hey, do you reckon that's where the warrior's gone back to?

THE DOCTOR: Well, he didn't come by Shetland pony, Jamie.

THE ICE WARRIORS

'It's funny, because people back home think that space travel's going to be all whizzing about and teleports and anti-gravity, but it's not, is it? It's tough.'

ROSE, *THE IMPOSSIBLE PLANET*

'The wonderful world of space travel. The prettier it looks, the more likely it is to kill you.'

RILEY, *42*

'There's a lot of things you need to get across this universe. Warp drive, wormhole refractors. You know the thing you need most of all? You need a hand to hold.'

THE DOCTOR, *FEAR HER*

ADVENTURE

'Rest is for the weary, sleep is for the dead!'

THE DOCTOR, *ATTACK OF THE CYBERMEN*

'Yes, it all started out as a mild curiosity in a junkyard, and now it's turned out to be... quite a great spirit of adventure, don't you think?'

THE DOCTOR, *THE SENSORITES*

THE DOCTOR: Ah, you want me to volunteer. Isn't that it?

THE WHITE GUARDIAN: Precisely.

THE DOCTOR: And if I don't?

THE WHITE GUARDIAN: Nothing.

THE DOCTOR: Nothing? You mean nothing will happen to me?

THE WHITE GUARDIAN: Nothing at all... ever.

THE RIBOS OPERATION

TEGAN: Anything could be out there.

THE DOCTOR: Yes, and going out is the only way to learn what it is.

ENLIGHTENMENT

'I was imparting a little information. When you ask a question, you should listen to the answer, my girl, otherwise, you will gain absolutely no benefit from being in my company. It is the province of knowledge to speak, and the privilege of wisdom to listen.'

THE DOCTOR, *THE TWO DOCTORS*

MEL: There's the swimming pool, right at the very top of the building. Oh, it's wonderful. I can't wait to have a dip in that. Paradise Towers, here we come.

THE DOCTOR: That's the problem with young people today, no spirit of adventure.

PARADISE TOWERS

'Number one rule of the intergalactic explorer, Doctor. If you hear somebody talking about good vibes and letting it all hang out, run a mile.'

CAPTAIN COOK, *THE GREATEST SHOW IN THE GALAXY*

'And you go with him, that wonderful Doctor. You go and see the stars, and then bring a bit of them back for your old Gramps.'

WILF, *THE POISON SKY*

BEN: Oh, of all the bloomin' fixes to be in.

POLLY: I don't know. I find it pretty exciting.

BEN: Oh, you would.

THE SMUGGLERS

THE DOCTOR: Where's your spirit of adventure?

IAN: It died a slow and painful death when those bats came out of the rafters!

THE CHASE

'Because the thing is, Doctor, I believe it all now. You opened my eyes. All those amazing things out there, I believe them all. Well, apart from that replica of the *Titanic* flying over Buckingham Palace on Christmas Day. I mean, that's got to be a hoax.'

DONNA, *PARTNERS IN CRIME*

'The adventures come without us looking for them.'

BARBARA, *THE ROMANS*

ESCAPE

'There's always a way out. If only we can find it.'

THE DOCTOR, *THE ARMAGEDDON FACTOR*

THE DOCTOR: Right, shouldn't be too far down. Just put your arms over your head, and slide.

PERI: What happens if I get stuck?

THE DOCTOR: I shouldn't advise that. I'll be right behind you.

THE TWO DOCTORS

'The moral is, if you're going to get stuck at the end of the universe, get stuck with an ex-Time Agent and his Vortex manipulator.'

CAPTAIN JACK HARKNESS, *THE SOUND OF DRUMS*

TEGAN: We've got to find the way out.

THE DOCTOR: Well, sometimes it's easier to look for the way in and then work backwards.

FRONTIOS

RORY: Ah, so this is the kind of escape plan where you survive about four seconds longer.

THE DOCTOR: What's wrong with four seconds? You can do loads in four seconds.

ASYLUM OF THE DALEKS

TEGAN: This is ridiculous, running about like rabbits in a hole. If you ask me—

THE DOCTOR: No one is, Tegan, so shush.

FRONTIOS

'Brigadier, I think our past is catching up on us. Or maybe it's our future. Come on, run!'

THE DOCTOR, *THE FIVE DOCTORS*

STRAX: And how will she locate the Doctor?

VASTRA: To find him, she needs only ignore all keep-out signs, go through every locked door, and run towards any form of danger that presents itself.

STRAX: Business as usual, then.

THE CRIMSON HORROR

'There's only one thing we can do… Run!'

THE DOCTOR, *THE SPACE PIRATES*

THE DOCTOR: We can't keep doing this.

RIVER: Any ideas?

THE DOCTOR: Yeah, the usual. Run!

THE ANGELS TAKE MANHATTAN

TEGAN: You mean you're deliberately choosing to go on the run from your own people in a rackety old TARDIS?

THE DOCTOR: Why not? After all, that's how it all started.

THE FIVE DOCTORS

AND IF ALL
ELSE FAILS...

JAMIE: Have you thought up some clever plan, Doctor?

THE DOCTOR: Yes, Jamie, I believe I have.

JAMIE: What are you going to do?

THE DOCTOR: Bung a rock at it.

THE ABOMINABLE SNOWMEN

Chapter Six:
The Tools

'If you have a tool,
it's stupid not to use it.'

THE DOCTOR, *INFERNO*

THE SONIC SCREWDRIVER

'It's a sonic screwdriver. Never fails. There we are. Neat isn't it? All done by sound waves.'

THE DOCTOR, *FURY FROM THE DEEP*

JACK: Who looks at a screwdriver and thinks, ooh, this could be a little more sonic?

THE DOCTOR: What, you've never been bored? ... Never had a long night? Never had a lot of cabinets to put up?

THE DOCTOR DANCES

'Harmless is just the word. That's why I like it. Doesn't kill, doesn't wound, doesn't maim. But I'll tell you what it does do. It is very good at opening doors.'

THE DOCTOR, *DOOMSDAY*

DONNA: Sonic it! Use the thingy!

THE DOCTOR: I can't. It's wood!

DONNA: What, it doesn't do wood?!

SILENCE IN THE LIBRARY

MARTHA: What's that thing?

THE DOCTOR: Sonic screwdriver.

MARTHA: Well, if you're not going to answer me properly.

THE DOCTOR: No, really, it is. It's a screwdriver, and it's sonic. Look.

MARTHA: What else have you got, a laser spanner?

THE DOCTOR: I did, but it was stolen by Emily Pankhurst, cheeky woman.

SMITH AND JONES

AMY: That is breaking and entering.

THE DOCTOR: What did I break? Sonicing and entering. Totally different.

THE HUNGRY EARTH

'Why are you pointing your screwdrivers like that? They're scientific instruments, not water pistols.'

THE WAR DOCTOR, *THE DAY OF THE DOCTOR*

JACK: OK. This can function as a sonic blaster, a sonic cannon, and as a triple-enfolded sonic disrupter. Doc, what you got?

THE DOCTOR: I've got a sonic, er. Oh, never mind.

JACK: What?

THE DOCTOR: It's sonic, OK? Let's leave it at that.

JACK: Disrupter? Cannon? What?

THE DOCTOR: It's sonic! Totally sonic! I am soniced up!

JACK: A sonic what?!

THE DOCTOR: Screwdriver!

THE DOCTOR DANCES

'Word of advice. If you're attacking a man with a sonic screwdriver, don't let him near the sound system.'

THE DOCTOR, *THE RUNAWAY BRIDE*

'Know what's interesting about my screwdriver? Very hard to interfere with. Practically nothing's strong enough. Well, some hairdryers, but I'm working on that.'

THE DOCTOR, *FOREST OF THE DEAD*

'Even the sonic screwdriver won't get me out of this one.'

THE DOCTOR, *THE INVASION OF TIME*

WHEN SONICS ARE DESTROYED

'I feel as though you've just killed an old friend.'

THE DOCTOR, *THE VISITATION*

'I loved my sonic screwdriver.'

THE DOCTOR, *SMITH AND JONES*

K-9 – A TIME LORD'S (SECOND) BEST FRIEND

THE DOCTOR: Would you like a ball bearing?

K-9: Please do not mock, master.

THE INVASION OF TIME

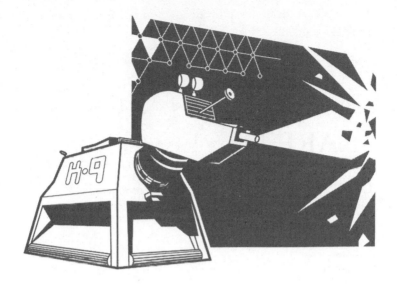

RIGG: What's that?

THE DOCTOR: Oh, K-9? Well, a computer of sorts.

RIGG: It looks more like a dog. Does he bark?

THE DOCTOR: No. But he has been known to bite.

NIGHTMARE OF EDEN

PROFESSOR MARIUS: That tin thing is my best friend and constant companion. He's a computer. You see, on Earth, I always used to have a dog. But up here, the weight penalty, well, it's just not possible. So I had K-9 made up. He's very useful. He's my own personal data bank. He knows everything that I do, don't you, K-9?

K-9: Affirmative, and more, master.

THE INVISIBLE ENEMY

'K-9 seems to have made up his own mind. I only hope he's TARDIS trained.'

PROFESSOR MARIUS, *THE INVISIBLE ENEMY*

THE DOCTOR: An assistant? Please, sir, on an assignment like this, I'd much rather work alone. In my experience, assistants mean trouble. I have to protect them and show them and teach them and – Couldn't I just... couldn't I just manage with K-9?

THE WHITE GUARDIAN: K-9 is a mere machine.

THE DOCTOR: He's a very sensitive machine!

THE RIBOS OPERATION

K-9: Satisfactory, mistress?

LEELA: Yes, K-9. What do you want, a biscuit?

THE SUN MAKERS

THE DOCTOR: K-9, I don't know how to say this, K-9.

K-9: Master, your concern is noted. Please do not embarrass me.

THE DOCTOR: Good dog.

THE SUN MAKERS

K-9: Predict only sixty per cent chance of success, master.

THE DOCTOR: Tell me, K-9, how is it you always look on the black side of things? Here am I, trying a little lateral thinking, and what do you do? You trample all over it with logic.

NIGHTMARE OF EDEN

THE DOCTOR: We all make mistakes sometimes, don't we, K-9?

K-9: Negative.

THE ARMAGEDDON FACTOR

'K-9, sulking is also an emotional thing. If you cannot wish, you cannot sulk.'

LEELA, *THE INVASION OF TIME*

THE DOCTOR: They can read thoughts. Even encephalographic patterns. That's why I've plugged K-9 into the Matrix instead of me. He's got no brains, you see. Sorry about that, K-9.

ANDRED: Can you trust a machine?

THE DOCTOR: This one I can. He's my second best friend.

THE INVASION OF TIME

K-9: The accuracy of this unit has deteriorated below zero utility.

ADRIC: You mean you're worse than useless.

K-9: Affirmative.

WARRIORS' GATE

THE DOCTOR: Ion drive, or I'm a budgie's cousin.

K-9: Affirmative ion drive. Family grouping negative.

UNDERWORLD

K-9: You have triggered the primary alert function.

THE DOCTOR: Blast!

K-9: Affirmative.

THE ARMAGEDDON FACTOR

'Batteries my exhausted nearly are…'

K-9, *THE PIRATE PLANET*

'Intentions unknown. Hypothesis unfriendly, as K-9 would say.'

THE DOCTOR, *KINDA*

COMPUTERS

'The trouble with computers, of course, is that they're very sophisticated idiots. They do exactly what you tell them at amazing speed, even if you order them to kill you. So if you do happen to change your mind, it's very difficult to stop them obeying the original order, but… not impossible.'

THE DOCTOR, *ROBOT*

'Now, the best thing about a machine that makes sense, you can very easily make it turn out nonsense.'

THE DOCTOR, *THE TOMB OF THE CYBERMEN*

MISS GARRETT: Here we are completely computerised.

THE DOCTOR: Well, never mind.

THE ICE WARRIORS

CLENT: You've worked with computers, I presume?

THE DOCTOR: Ah, only when I have to.

THE ICE WARRIORS

LEELA: What is it?

THE DOCTOR: Number two control room has been closed for redecoration. I don't like the colour.

LEELA: White isn't a colour.

THE DOCTOR: That's the trouble with computers. Always think in black and white. No aquamarines, no blues, no imagination.

THE INVISIBLE ENEMY

'You're still nothing but a gigantic adding machine like every other computer.'

THE DOCTOR, *THE GREEN DEATH*

ROMANA: Well, at least on Gallifrey we can capture a good likeness. Computers can draw.

THE DOCTOR: What? Computer pictures? You sit in Paris and talk of computer pictures?

CITY OF DEATH

HADE: To err is computer.

THE DOCTOR: To forgive is fine?

THE SUN MAKERS

JO: A mind probe?

THE DOCTOR: Oh, you don't want to worry about those things, Jo. As long as you tell them the truth, they can't do you any harm… Well, they're only sort of computers with a few extra knobs on. And you know how stupid computers can be, don't you?

FRONTIER IN SPACE

LEELA: You did say he was the most powerful computer ever built.

THE DOCTOR Yes, and very charming he is too when he wants to be. Marvellous host. I remember once at one of his dinner parties…

LEELA: Doctor, he just tried to kill you!

THE FACE OF EVIL

'Even simple one-dimensional chess exposes the limitations of the machine mind.'

THE DOCTOR, *THE SUN MAKERS*

'Everything in life has its purpose, Drathro. Every creature plays its part. But the purpose of life is too big to be knowable. A million computers couldn't solve that one.'

THE DOCTOR, *THE TRIAL OF A TIME LORD: THE MYSTERIOUS PLANET*

I, ROBOT

'Mankind is not worthy to survive. Once it is destroyed, I shall build more machines like myself. Machines do not lie.'

ROBOT K-1, *ROBOT*

ZADEK: You can't trust androids, you know.

THE DOCTOR: That's funny, you know. That's what some androids say about people.

THE ANDROIDS OF TARA

SARAH: Oh, it's got a brain, hasn't it? It walks and talks like us. How can you be sure it doesn't have feelings too? Are you all right?

ROBOT K-1: My functioning is unimpaired.

SARAH: But you were distressed. I saw that.

ROBOT K-1: Conflict with my prime directive causes imbalance in my neural circuits.

SARAH: I'm sorry. It wasn't my idea.

ROBOT K-1: The imbalance has been corrected. It is not logical that you should feel sorrow.

MISS WINTERS: Really, Miss Smith, this is absurd. I think you must be the sort of girl that gives motorcars pet names.

ROBOT

DRATHRO: I know of values. Is your point that organics are of more value than robots?

THE DOCTOR: Yes. If you want to look at it that way.

DRATHRO: Then why should I be in command of organics if they are of greater value?

THE DOCTOR: But without organics there wouldn't be any robots. There'd be no one to create them.

DRATHRO: Accepted. This shows that robots are more advanced, therefore of more value.

THE TRIAL OF A TIME LORD: THE MYSTERIOUS PLANET

'Robots don't have feelings. It's the people they serve we must hope are friendly.'

THE DOCTOR, *THE ROBOTS OF DEATH*

'You know, people never really lose that feeling of unease with robots. The more of them there are, the greater the unease and of course the greater the dependence. It's a vicious circle. People can neither live with them nor exist without them.'

THE DOCTOR, *THE ROBOTS OF DEATH*

#DOCTORWHO

'You two! We're at the end of the universe, all right? Right at the edge of knowledge itself and you're busy blogging!'

THE DOCTOR, *UTOPIA*

THE DOCTOR: This whole world is swimming in wifi. We're living in a wifi soup. Suppose something got inside it. Suppose there was something living in the wifi, harvesting human minds. Extracting them. Imagine that. Human souls trapped like flies in the worldwide web. Stuck forever, crying out for help.

CLARA: Isn't that basically Twitter?

THE BELLS OF SAINT JOHN

'I bring you to a paradise planet, two billion light years from Earth, and you want to update Twitter.'

THE DOCTOR, *THE GIRL WHO WAITED*

TRANSPORTS OF DELIGHT

'This planet is going to be destroyed and I'm stuck in a traffic jam.'

THE DOCTOR, *DOCTOR WHO* (TV MOVIE)

'We don't walk away. But when we're holding on to something precious, we run. We run and run, fast as we can and we don't stop running until we are out from under the shadow.'

THE DOCTOR, *THE RINGS OF AKHATEN*

ROMANA: For every action, there is an equal and opposite reaction.

THE DOCTOR: That's right.

ROMANA: So Newton invented punting.

THE DOCTOR: Oh, yes. There was no limit to Isaac's genius.

SHADA

ADRIC: So what is a railway station?

THE DOCTOR: Well, a place where one embarks and disembarks from compartments on wheels, drawn along these rails by a steam engine. Rarely on time.

NYSSA: What a very silly activity.

THE DOCTOR: You think so? As a boy I always wanted to drive one.

BLACK ORCHID

'Horse, you have failed in your mission. We are lost, with no sign of Sweetville. Do you have any final words before your summary execution? The usual story. Fourth one this week, and I'm not even hungry.'

STRAX, *THE CRIMSON HORROR*

URCHIN: Turn around when possible. Then, at the end of the road, turn right… bear left for a quarter of a mile and you will have reached your destination.

STRAX: Thank you. What is your name?

URCHIN: Thomas, sir. Thomas Thomas.

STRAX: I think you will do well, Thomas Thomas.

THE CRIMSON HORROR

'And you've got an office on a train. That is so cool. Can I have an office? Never had an office before. Or a train. Or a train-slash-office.'

THE DOCTOR, *THE WEDDING OF RIVER SONG*

MAN: Really, Doctor. A motorbike? Hardly seems like you.

THE DOCTOR: I rode this in the Antigrav Olympics, 2074. I came last.

MAN: The building is in lock-down. I'm afraid you're not coming in.

THE DOCTOR: Did you even hear the word 'antigrav'?

THE BELLS OF SAINT JOHN

SCIENCE AND SCIENTISTS

KALMAR: Doctor? That's a word I've seen in the old records. It's a title used by scientists. Are you a scientist, Doctor, like me?

THE DOCTOR: Well, I've dabbled a bit.

STATE OF DECAY

'We were just wondering if there were any other scientists… You know, witch-wiggler, wangateur. Fortune teller? Mundunugu?'

THE DOCTOR, *STATE OF DECAY*

'Like many scientists, I'm afraid the Rani simply sees us as walking heaps of chemicals. There's no place for the soul in her scheme of things.'

THE DOCTOR, *THE MARK OF THE RANI*

'I had all I can take of that cant in our university days. Am I expected to abandon my research because of the side effects on inferior species? Are you prepared to abandon walking in case you squash an insect underfoot?'

THE RANI, *TIME AND THE RANI*

JANO: I am sorry you take this attitude, Doctor. It is most unscientific. You are standing in the way of human progress.

THE DOCTOR: Human progress, sir? How dare you call your treatment of these people progress!

THE SAVAGES

JANO: We have achieved a very great deal merely by the sacrifice of a few savages.

THE DOCTOR: The sacrifice of even one soul is far too great! You must put an end to this inhuman practice.

THE SAVAGES

ZAROFF: So you're just a little man after all, Doctor, like all the rest. You disappoint me.

THE DOCTOR: You disappoint me, Professor. I didn't think a man of science needed the backing of thugs.

THE UNDERWATER MENACE

PROFESSOR RUMFORD: I warn you, Doctor, he doesn't like scientists.

THE DOCTOR: Well, very few people do, in my experience.

THE STONES OF BLOOD

'There is a difference between serious scientific investigation and meddling.'

THE DOCTOR, *KINDA*

KNIGHT: What's a girl like you doing in a job like this?

ANNE: Well, when I was a little girl I thought I'd like to be a scientist, so I became a scientist.

KNIGHT: Just like that?

ANNE: Just like that.

THE WEB OF FEAR

MISS WINTERS: I suppose it all seems very elementary to a scientist of your standing, Doctor.

THE DOCTOR: Yes, it does rather, but never mind. You've got to start somewhere.

ROBOT

TODD: Which way?

THE DOCTOR: Has anyone ever told you, you ask a lot of questions?

TODD: It's my training. I'm a scientist.

KINDA

'You and I are scientists, Professor. We buy our privilege to experiment at the cost of total responsibility.'

THE DOCTOR, *PLANET OF EVIL*

'Eureka's Greek for this bath is too hot.'

THE DOCTOR, *THE TALONS OF WENG-CHIANG*

KERENSKY: You are stretching me to the limit, Count.

SCARLIONI: Only thus is true progress ever made. You, as a scientist, should be the first to appreciate that.

CITY OF DEATH

KETTLEWELL: For years I have been trying to persuade people to stop spoiling this planet, Doctor. Now, with the help of my friends, I can make them.

THE DOCTOR: Aren't you forgetting that in science, as in morality, the end never justifies the means?

ROBOT

SCIENCE VERSUS MAGIC

'I too used to believe in magic, but the Doctor has taught me about science. It is better to believe in science.'

LEELA, *HORROR OF FANG ROCK*

'The greatest raiding cruiser ever built. And I built it, Mr Fibuli, I built it with technology so far advanced you would not be able to distinguish it from magic.'

THE CAPTAIN, *THE PIRATE PLANET*

THE DOCTOR: What is Clarke's law?

ACE: Any advanced form of technology is indistinguishable from magic.

THE DOCTOR: Well, the reverse is true.

ACE: Any advanced form of magic is indistinguishable from technology.

BATTLEFIELD

'It's not my fault if a bunch of backward savages have turned a Magnum Mark VII light converter into a totem pole!'

SABALOM GLITZ, *THE TRIAL OF A TIME LORD: THE MYSTERIOUS PLANET*

JO: But it really is the dawning of the age of Aquarius... you know, the supernatural and all that magic bit.

THE DOCTOR: You know, really, Jo, I'm obviously wasting my time trying to turn you into a scientist.

THE DAEMONS

'Yes, superstition is a strange thing, my dear, but sometimes it tells the truth.'

THE DOCTOR, *THE SMUGGLERS*

'Everything that happens in life must have a scientific explanation. If you know where to look for it, that is.'

THE DOCTOR, *THE DAEMONS*

JO: How did you do that?

THE DOCTOR: Iron. It's an old magical defence.

JO: But you don't believe in magic.

THE DOCTOR: I don't, but he did. Luckily.

THE DAEMONS

MARTHA: But is it real, though? I mean, witches, black magic and all that, it's real?

THE DOCTOR: Course it isn't!

MARTHA: Well, how am I supposed to know? I've only just started believing in time travel. Give me a break.

THE SHAKESPEARE CODE

THE DOCTOR: I named her. The power of a name. That's old magic.

MARTHA: But there's no such thing as magic.

THE DOCTOR: Well, it's just a different sort of science. You lot, you chose mathematics. Given the right string of numbers, the right equation, you can split the atom. Carrionites use words instead.

SHAKESPEARE: Use them for what?

THE DOCTOR: The end of the world.

THE SHAKESPEARE CODE

'The Minyans thought of us as gods, you see, which was all very flattering and we were new at space-time exploration, so we thought we could help. We gave them medical and scientific aid, better communications, better weapons … Kicked us out at gunpoint. Then they went to war with each other, learnt how to split the atom, discovered the toothbrush and finally split the planet.'

THE DOCTOR, *UNDERWORLD*

MACHINES THAT GO 'DING'

'Tracked you down with this. This is my timey-wimey detector. It goes 'ding' when there's stuff. Also, it can boil an egg at thirty paces – whether you want it to or not, actually, so I've learned to stay away from hens. It's not pretty when they blow.'

THE DOCTOR, *BLINK*

'It's a machine that goes 'ding'. Made it myself. Lights up in the presence of shape-shifter DNA. Oooh. Also it can microwave frozen dinners from up to twenty feet and download comics from the future. I never know when to stop.'

THE DOCTOR, *THE DAY OF THE DOCTOR*

'Never trust gimmicky gadgets.'

THE DOCTOR, *THE PIRATE PLANET*

'It's for measuring time on 19 different planets ... Oh, it can also be used for modifying dythrambic oscillations, cleaning your shoes, sharpening pencils. It can even peel your apples.'

THE DOCTOR, *THE RIBOS OPERATION*

'Oh! Oh, look. Oh, lovely. The ACR 99821. Oh, bliss. Nice action on the toggle switches. You know, I do love a toggle switch. Actually, I like the word toggle. Nice noun. Excellent verb. Oi, don't mess with the settings.'

THE DOCTOR, *HIDE*

WHEN TECHNOLOGY GOES WRONG

YATES: Doctor, suppose this gadget of yours doesn't work?

THE DOCTOR: Then I shall simply turn round and come back, feeling rather foolish.

INVASION OF THE DINOSAURS

THE DOCTOR: Can I get a map of London on this thing? …

CORNISH: That machine will give you surface maps of every surveyed planet, but a map of London? No.

THE DOCTOR: Useless gadgets.

THE AMBASSADORS OF DEATH

THE DOCTOR: What about the colony ship? Must have been brimming with gadgetry.

RANGE: Oh, systems that could rebuild a civilisation for us. Failure-proof technology.

THE DOCTOR: What happened to it all?

RANGE: It failed.

FRONTIOS

'I hate those transmat things. Like travelling in a food mixer, and just as dangerous. I'd be afraid of coming out puréed.'

TEGAN, *MAWDRYN UNDEAD*

'Captain. Your magnifactoid eccentricolometer is definitely on the blink.'

THE DOCTOR, *THE PIRATE PLANET*

'If there's anyone in the emergency control room, would you please answer the phone. Thank you.'

PA, *DRAGONFIRE*

LAWRENCE: You're not proposing to dismantle a piece of equipment worth fifteen million pounds with a screwdriver?

THE DOCTOR: Well, it's not worth fifteen million pins if it doesn't work, is it?

DOCTOR WHO AND THE SILURIANS

THE DOCTOR: Macrovectoid particle analyser. Omnimodular thermocron – there! Megaphoton discharge link.'

PRALIX: What do we do?

THE DOCTOR: Hit it!

THE PIRATE PLANET

ORCINI: We prefer to stand.

KARA: Of course. How foolish. As men of action, you must be like coiled springs, alert, ready to pounce.

ORCINI: Nothing so romantic. I have an artificial leg with a faulty hydraulic valve. When seated, the valve is inclined to jam.

REVELATION OF THE DALEKS

ROSE: Where I come from, Jackie doesn't know how to work the timer on the video recorder.

PETE: I showed her that last week... Point taken.

FATHER'S DAY

'You can't always go by the manuals.'

THE DOCTOR, *FULL CIRCLE*

LEELA: K-9's breaking up, my blaster's finished. What are we going to do?

THE DOCTOR: Shall we try using our intelligence?

LEELA: Well, if you think that's a good idea.

THE INVISIBLE ENEMY

ROMANA: What about the Mandrels? You won't have K-9 or a gun.

THE DOCTOR: I'll have to use my wits.

NIGHTMARE OF EDEN

THE BRIGADIER: Twenty thousand pounds of UNIT money gone up in a puff of smoke.

THE DOCTOR: You've got the mind of an accountant, Lethbridge-Stewart.

THE DAEMONS

LOGIC

'Logic, my dear Zoe, merely enables one to be wrong with authority.'

THE DOCTOR, *THE WHEEL IN SPACE*

'There's too much I don't know. I was trained to believe logic and calculation would provide me with all the answers. I'm just beginning to realise there are questions which I can't answer … What good am I? I've been created for some false kind of existence where only known kinds of emergencies are catered for. Well, what good is that to me now?'

ZOE, *THE WHEEL IN SPACE*

DRATHRO: I have a learning capacity, but my processes of ratiocination are logical. Organics often eliminate such steps.

THE DOCTOR: It's called intuition.

THE TRIAL OF A TIME LORD: THE MYSTERIOUS PLANET

SCOTT: I haven't had much experience of fighting androids.

THE DOCTOR: Oh, they're just like people.

NYSSA: Only they function much more logically.

THE DOCTOR: Which can be their weakness.

EARTHSHOCK

THE DOCTOR: All elephants are pink. Nellie is an elephant, therefore Nellie is pink. Logical?

DAVROS: Perfectly.

THE DOCTOR: You know what a human would say to that?

DAVROS: What?

TYSSAN: Elephants aren't pink.

DESTINY OF THE DALEKS

BAFFLEGAB

'Bafflegab, my dear. I've never heard such bafflegab in all my lives!'

THE DOCTOR, *THE PIRATE PLANET*

THE DOCTOR: With a little bit of jiggery-pokery…

ROSE: Is that a technical term, jiggery-pokery?

THE DOCTOR: Yeah, I came first in jiggery-pokery, what about you?

ROSE: No, I failed hullabaloo.

THE END OF THE WORLD

OSGOOD: What's the principle, sir?

THE DOCTOR: Negative diathermy, Sergeant. Buffer the molecular movement of the air with the reverse-phase short waves. It's quite simple.

OSGOOD: Simple? It's impossible.

THE DOCTOR: Yes, well, according to classical aerodynamics, it's impossible for a bumblebee to fly!

THE DAEMONS

THE DOCTOR: Suppose I reflect a transmission beam off the security shield, feed it back through a link crystal bank and boost it through the transducer?

K-9: Couldn't have put it better myself, master.

THE DOCTOR: I don't think you could.

THE INVASION OF TIME

GRAVIS: I should like to see it, this TARDIS.

THE DOCTOR: Well, it's not all here at the moment, you understand. It's, er, it's been spatially distributed to optimise the, er, the packing efficiency of, er, the real-time envelope.

FRONTIOS

THE DOCTOR: I've switched the Captain's circuits around to create a hyperspatial force shield around the shrunken planets, then I put his dematerialisation control into remote mode … first I dematerialise the TARDIS, then I make Zanak dematerialise for a millisecond or two, then I invert the gravity field of the hyperspatial forceshield and drop the shrunken planets…

ROMANA: Into the hollow centre of Zanak!

THE DOCTOR: Exactly.

ROMANA: What then?

THE DOCTOR: Well, I would have thought that was perfectly obvious.

THE PIRATE PLANET

THE DOCTOR: Right, well tell him to build an EHF wide-bandwidth variable-phase oscillator, with a negative feedback circuit tuneable to the frequency of an air molecule at, um, what is the temperature up at the barrier, Brigadier?

THE BRIGADIER: We've no idea what you're talking about, Doctor. Over.

THE DAEMONS

'Well, I've reversed the polarity of the neutron flow, so the TARDIS should be free of the force field now.'

THE DOCTOR, *THE FIVE DOCTORS*

'New technology dates so quickly these days.'

THE DOCTOR, *THE KEEPER OF TRAKEN*

Chapter Seven:
The Simple Things

'For some people, small, beautiful events is what life is all about!'

THE DOCTOR, *EARTHSHOCK*

APPRECIATING BEAUTY

'Better to go hungry than starve for beauty.'

CAMECA, *THE AZTECS*

'Good looks are no substitute for a sound character.'

THE DOCTOR, *THE PIRATE PLANET*

COUNTESS: I was rather under the impression that Mr Duggan was following me.

THE DOCTOR: Ah. Well, you're a beautiful woman, probably, and Duggan was trying to summon up the courage to ask you out to dinner…

CITY OF DEATH

THE LITTLE PEOPLE

SARAH: I know we're not important …

THE DOCTOR: Who said you're not important? I've travelled to all sorts of places, done things you couldn't even imagine, but you two. Street corner, two in the morning, getting a taxi home. I've never had a life like that. Yes. I'll try and save you.

FATHER'S DAY

'You shouldn't feel ashamed of your grief. It's right to grieve. Your Bert, he was unique. In the whole history of the world, there's never been anybody just like Bert. And there'll never be another, even if the world lasts for a hundred million centuries.'

CLIFFORD JONES, *THE GREEN DEATH*

'Planets and history and stuff. That's what we do. But not today. No. Today, we're answering a cry for help from the scariest place in the universe. A child's bedroom.'

THE DOCTOR, *NIGHT TERRORS*

RELAXATION

'Relax. Relax. More haste, more waste. Pleasure is beautiful.'

THE DOCTOR, *THE MACRA TERROR*

'For me – as for you, sir – sleep is sometimes better nourishment than good red meat.'

THE PORTREEVE, *CASTROVALVA*

'Stupid expression, stands to reason. Why doesn't it lie down to reason? Much easier to reason lying down. Relaxes the cerebellum.'

THE DOCTOR, *THE CREATURE FROM THE PIT*

SANDERS: We've been having fun.

THE DOCTOR: Have you? Oh, good. There's nothing quite like it, is there?

KINDA

GENERAL ADVICE

'Never underestimate plumbing. Plumbing's very important.'

THE DOCTOR, *THE LONG GAME*

'Never trust a man with dirty fingernails.'

THE DOCTOR, *THE TALONS OF WENG-CHIANG*

'Never be certain of anything. It's a sign of weakness.'

THE DOCTOR, *THE FACE OF EVIL*

'Never throw anything away, Harry. Where's my 500-year diary? I remember jotting some notes on the Sontarans. It's a mistake to clutter one's pockets, Harry.'

THE DOCTOR, *THE SONTARAN EXPERIMENT*

'Long acquaintance is no guarantee for honesty.'

THE DOCTOR, *THE DALEKS' MASTER PLAN*

'Nothing's just rubbish if you have an enquiring mind.'

THE DOCTOR, *THE INVASION OF TIME*

'Don't be cool, guys. Cool is not cool.'

THE DOCTOR, *THE TIME OF THE DOCTOR*

'You give a monkey control of its environment, it'll fill the world with bananas.'

THE DOCTOR, *THE TWO DOCTORS*

'If people see you mean them no harm, they never hurt you. Nine times out of ten.'

THE DOCTOR, *THE ROBOTS OF DEATH*

'People who talk about infallibility are usually on very shaky ground.'

THE DOCTOR, *THE MIND OF EVIL*

'When replacing a brain, always make sure the arrow A is pointing to the front.'

THE DOCTOR, *DESTINY OF THE DALEKS*

'Oh, you should always waste time when you don't have any. Time is not the boss of you. Rule four hundred and eight.'

THE DOCTOR, *LET'S KILL HITLER*

'Don't get into a spaceship with a madman. Didn't anyone ever teach you that?'

THE DOCTOR, *JOURNEY TO THE CENTRE OF THE TARDIS*

'Never trust a Venusian shanghorn with a perigosto stick.'

THE DOCTOR, *THE GREEN DEATH*

'Rash action is worse than no action at all.'

THE DOCTOR, *THE EDGE OF DESTRUCTION*

'Don't be a monk. Monks are not cool.'

THE DOCTOR, *THE BELLS OF SAINT JOHN*

'Never ignore a coincidence. Unless you're busy. In which case, always ignore a coincidence.'

THE DOCTOR, *THE PANDORICA OPENS*

'An interested mind brooks no delay.'

CAMECA, *THE AZTECS*

'Don't just be obedient. Always make up your own mind.'

THE DOCTOR, *THE MACRA TERROR*

'Never guess. Unless you have to. There's enough uncertainty in the universe as it is.'

THE DOCTOR, *LOGOPOLIS*

'An apple a day keeps the, er… No, never mind.'

THE DOCTOR, *KINDA*

SHOPPING

'I like the little shop.'

THE DOCTOR, *NEW EARTH*

MEL: A freezer centre? How boring.

THE DOCTOR: Oh, trust not to appearances, Mel. You never know what might be lurking in the freezer chests. Think gothic.

DRAGONFIRE

LANG: I thank you for your offer, Doctor, but frankly, I find you unreliable.

THE DOCTOR: So's most currency. Doesn't stop people spending money wisely.

THE TWIN DILEMMA

'Oh, look down there, you've got a little shop. I like a little shop.'

THE DOCTOR, *SMITH AND JONES*

DONNA: Are we safe here?

THE DOCTOR: Of course we're safe. There's a little shop.

SILENCE IN THE LIBRARY

'I'm the Doctor. I work in a shop now. Here to help. Look, they gave me a badge with my name on in case I forget who I am. Very thoughtful, as that does happen.'

THE DOCTOR, *CLOSING TIME*

HIGH FABSION

FIRE ESCAPE: You we like, Doctor. What you wear is high fabsion and ice hot, for an old one.

THE DOCTOR: Oh, thank you very much. But clothes don't maketh the man, you know.

PARADISE TOWERS

'Bow ties are cool.'

THE DOCTOR, *THE ELEVENTH HOUR*

RIVER: What in the name of sanity have you got on your head?

THE DOCTOR: It's a fez. I wear a fez now. Fezzes are cool.

THE BIG BANG

'I wear a Stetson now. Stetsons are cool.'

THE DOCTOR, *THE IMPOSSIBLE ASTRONAUT*

THE DOCTOR: Ah, there you are, both of you. Well, I don't think I was so far wrong, my boy. What do I look like, my dear?

DODO: You're really with it now, Doctor.

THE DOCTOR: Yes. With what, my dear?

THE SAVAGES

'I don't like this jacket. Not very comfortable. I like a jacket with a lot of pockets, don't you?'

THE DOCTOR, *THE SUN MAKERS*

'Brave choice, celery, but fair play to you. Not a lot of men can carry off a decorative vegetable.'

THE DOCTOR, *TIME CRASH*

'Is nobody going to mention Rory's ponytail? You hold him down, I'll cut it off?'

THE DOCTOR, *AMY'S CHOICE*

'Nothing on Earth changes quite so often as the fashion. You wouldn't believe the way some people look. Some of them even wear safety pins.'

THE DOCTOR, *FOUR TO DOOMSDAY*

POLLY: Hey, you've got your own clothes back.

THE DOCTOR: Yes. Can you imagine, I found them thrown out on the rubbish dump, behind the inn.

BEN: Amazing, isn't it? Well, mine should be dry by now.

POLLY: I liked you better in your dress, Doctor.

KIRSTY: Aye, you made a good granny.

THE HIGHLANDERS

THE DOCTOR: Let's have your tie.

IAN: Well, I haven't got one.

THE DOCTOR: I know you're not wearing one, dear boy, but the one round your middle, hmm?

IAN: I hope my pants stay up.

THE DOCTOR: Yes, well, that's your affair, not mine.

THE WEB PLANET

'Well, you please yourself, I'm no fashion expert.'

THE DOCTOR, *THE STONES OF BLOOD*

'Beau Brummell always said I looked better in a cloak.'

THE DOCTOR, *THE SENSORITES*

PERI: You can't go out dressed like that.

THE DOCTOR: Why ever not?

PERI: You look dreadful.

THE DOCTOR: My dear, that is what people said about Beau Brummell. Remember him?

PERI: Well, he had taste, a feeling for style.

THE DOCTOR: And I don't?

PERI: Not if what you're wearing is an example. It's, oh, *yuck*.

THE TWIN DILEMMA

THE DOCTOR: You look very nice in that dress, Victoria.

VICTORIA: Thank you. Don't you think it's a bit…

THE DOCTOR: A bit short? Oh, I shouldn't worry about that. Look at Jamie's!

THE TOMB OF THE CYBERMEN

'Oh, black tie. Whenever I wear this, something bad always happens.'

THE DOCTOR, *THE LAZARUS EXPERIMENT*

RORY: A poncho. The biggest crime against fashion since lederhosen.

AMY: Here we go. My boys. My poncho boys. If we're going to die, let's die looking like a Peruvian folk band.

AMY'S CHOICE

LEELA: These clothes are ridiculous. Why must I wear them?

THE DOCTOR: Because you can't go walking around Victorian London in skins. You'll frighten the horses.

THE TALONS OF WENG-CHIANG

REDVERS: Please, young lady, you're barely dressed.

ACE: Who's undressed?

THE DOCTOR: Excuse my young friend. She comes from a less civilised clime.

ACE: What do you want me to do, wrap up in a curtain?

THE DOCTOR: Be quiet, noble savage.

GHOST LIGHT

THE DOCTOR: Hey, where do you think you're going?

ROSE: 1860.

THE DOCTOR: Go out there dressed like that, you'll start a riot, Barbarella. There's a wardrobe through there. First left, second right, third on the left, go straight ahead, under the stairs, past the bins, fifth door on your left. Hurry up!

THE UNQUIET DEAD

THE DOCTOR: What do you think of that now, eh? A Viking helmet.

STEVEN: Oh, maybe.

THE DOCTOR: What do you mean, maybe? What do you think it is, a space helmet for a cow?

THE TIME MEDDLER

'I would like a hat like that.'

THE DOCTOR, *THE HIGHLANDERS*

ROMANA: I thought you said external appearances weren't important.

THE DOCTOR: Ah, but it's nice to get them right, though, isn't it?

DESTINY OF THE DALEKS

PHILOSOPHY

ASTRID: Oh, you're a Doctor?

THE DOCTOR: Well, not of any medical significance.

ASTRID: Doctor of law? Philosophy?

THE DOCTOR: Which law? Whose philosophies, eh?

THE ENEMY OF THE WORLD

ORCINI: It is rare for someone in my profession to meet a client on their home territory. Assassins, like debt collectors, are rarely welcome. When we are allowed on the premises, it's usually through the side door.

KARA: He is a philosopher. How charming.

REVELATION OF THE DALEKS

'Is a slave a slave if he doesn't know he's enslaved?'

THE EDITOR, *THE LONG GAME*

'Every problem has a solution.'

DALEK, *THE DALEKS*

'We're all just stories in the end.'

THE DOCTOR, *THE BIG BANG*

'Total takings for the day, one sandwich. Better than no sandwich, of course. Not as good as two sandwiches, or even a chicken.'

WEBLEY, *NIGHTMARE IN SILVER*

'The more you put things together, the more they keep falling apart, and that's the essence of the second law of thermodynamics and I never heard a truer word spoken.'

THE DOCTOR, *LOGOPOLIS*

'I get the impression they don't know where they're heading for. Come to that, do any of us?'

STIRLING, *THE REIGN OF TERROR*

'Everything has got to end some time, otherwise nothing would ever get started.'

THE DOCTOR, *A CHRISTMAS CAROL*

'To the rational mind, nothing is inexplicable, only unexplained.'

THE DOCTOR, *THE ROBOTS OF DEATH*

THE DOCTOR: Nothing's inexplicable.

RIGG: Then explain it!

THE DOCTOR: It's inexplicable.

NIGHTMARE OF EDEN

THE DOCTOR: Ignorance is – what's the opposite of bliss?

CLARA: Carlisle.

THE DOCTOR: Yes. Yes, Carlisle. Ignorance is Carlisle.

HIDE

'Leave the quotes to the expert, Mel!'

Following his sixth regeneration, the Doctor developed a knack for mangling quotes and proverbs. Here's just a selection from his first adventure, *Time and the Rani*.

A bull in a barber shop

Fit as a trombone

A bad workman always blames his fools

Absence makes the nose grow longer

A kangaroo never forgets

The proof of the pumpkin's in the squeezing

Where there's a will, there's a Tom, Dick and a Harriet

All good things come to a bend

Here's a turn-up for the cook

A bird in the hand keeps the Doctor away

Two wrongs don't make a left turn

A miss is as good as a smile

Time and tide melts the snowman

MUSIC

'All we can do now is think, and I think best to music. Now, where is my recorder?'

THE DOCTOR, *THE THREE DOCTORS*

'I should say, this isn't, you know, my whole life. It's not all spaceships and stuff, because I'm into all sorts of things. I like football. I like a drink. I like Spain. And if there's one thing I really, really love – then it's Jeff Lynne and the Electric Light Orchestra. Because you can't beat a bit of ELO.'

ELTON, *LOVE & MONSTERS*

THE DOCTOR: Where'd you learn to whistle?

DONNA: West Ham, every Saturday.

PLANET OF THE OOD

'You want to see Elvis, you go for the late fifties. The time before burgers. When they called him the Pelvis and he still had a waist. What's more, you see him in style.'

THE DOCTOR, *THE IDIOT'S LANTERN*

'Oh, yes. There are no other colours without the Blues.'

THE DOCTOR, *THE HAPPINESS PATROL*

'Klokleda partha menin klatch. Haroon, haroon, haroon. Klokleda sheena tirra nach. Haroon, haroon, haroon. Haroon, haroon, haroon. Haroon, haroon, haroon. Haroon, haroon, haroon. Haroon, haroon, haroon. Well, I must say, you seem quite partial to old Venusian lullabies, don't you, Aggedor, old chap, hmm?'

THE DOCTOR, *THE CURSE OF PELADON*

'It's the first line of an old Venusian lullaby, as a matter of fact. Roughly translated it goes, "Close your eyes, my darling. Well, three of them, at least."'

THE DOCTOR, *THE DAEMONS*

BOOKS AND STUFF

'Books are the principal business of a library, sir.'

SHARDOVAN, *CASTROVALVA*

'Reading's great. You like stories, George? Yeah? Me, too. When I was your age, about, ooh, a thousand years ago, I loved a good bedtime story. "The Three Little Sontarans". "The Emperor Dalek's New Clothes". "Snow White and the Seven Keys to Doomsday", eh? All the classics.'

THE DOCTOR, *NIGHT TERRORS*

'I enjoy the *Strand* magazine as much as the next man, but I am perfectly aware that Sherlock Holmes is a fictional character.'

DR SIMEON, *THE SNOWMEN*

'Books. People never really stop loving books. Fifty-first century. By now you've got holovids, direct-to-brain downloads, fiction mist. But you need the smell. The smell of books.'

THE DOCTOR, *SILENCE IN THE LIBRARY*

'If heroes don't exist, it is necessary to invent them. Good for public morale.'

BORUSA, *THE DEADLY ASSASSIN*

'Well, what's the use of a good quotation if you can't change it?'

THE DOCTOR, *THE TWO DOCTORS*

THE DOCTOR: I love biographies!

DONNA: Yeah, very you. Always a death at the end.

SILENCE IN THE LIBRARY

'You want weapons? We're in a library. Books! Best weapons in the world. This room's the greatest arsenal we could have.'

THE DOCTOR, *TOOTH AND CLAW*

TELEVISION

THE DOCTOR: You say you can't fit an enormous building into one of your smaller sitting rooms.

IAN: No.

THE DOCTOR: But you've discovered television, haven't you?

IAN: Yes.

THE DOCTOR: Then by showing an enormous building on your television screen, you can do what seemed impossible, couldn't you?

AN UNEARTHLY CHILD

THE DOCTOR: Improve what, for instance?

MONK: Well, for instance, Harold, King Harold, I know he'd be a good king. There wouldn't be all those wars in Europe, those claims over France went on for years and years. With peace the people would be able to better themselves. With a few hints and tips from me they'd be able to have jet airliners by 1320! Shakespeare would be able to put *Hamlet* on television.

THE DOCTOR: He'd do what?

MONK: The play *Hamlet* on television.

THE DOCTOR: Oh, yes, quite so, yes, of course, I do know the medium.

THE TIME MEDDLER

BENTON: What are we going to do now?

THE DOCTOR: Keep it confused. Feed it with useless information. I wonder if I have a television set handy.

THE THREE DOCTORS

ROSE: So history's happening and we're stuck here.

THE DOCTOR: Yes, we are …

ROSE: We could always do what everybody else does. We could watch it on TV.

ALIENS OF LONDON

'I hear they rot your brains. Rot them into soup. And your brain comes pouring out of your ears. That's what television does.'

GRAN, *THE IDIOT'S LANTERN*

WINSTANLEY: Are you one of these television chaps then?

THE DOCTOR: I am no sort of chap, sir.

WINSTANLEY: Forgive me, but I thought... Well, the costume and the wig, you know?

THE DAEMONS

THE ARTS

'But a theatre's magic, isn't it? You should know. Stand on this stage, say the right words with the right emphasis at the right time. Oh, you can make men weep, or cry with joy. Change them. You can change people's minds just with words in this place.'

THE DOCTOR, *THE SHAKESPEARE CODE*

'High drama is very similar to comedy. It's all a matter of timing.'

THE DOCTOR, *BATTLEFIELD*

DUGGAN: But it's a fake! You can't hang a fake Mona Lisa in the Louvre.

ROMANA: How can it be a fake if Leonardo painted it?

DUGGAN: With the words 'This is a fake' written under the paintwork in felt tip?

ROMANA: It doesn't affect what it looks like.

DUGGAN: It doesn't matter what it looks like.

THE DOCTOR: Doesn't it? Well, some people would say that's the whole point of painting.

CITY OF DEATH

A WELL-PREPARED MEAL

'I remember saying to old Napoleon. Boney, I said, always remember an army marches on its stomach.'

THE DOCTOR, *DAY OF THE DALEKS*

THE DOCTOR: When did you last have the pleasure of smelling a flower, watching a sunset, eating a well-prepared meal?

CYBERLEADER: These things are irrelevant.

EARTHSHOCK

'Anyone who likes jelly babies can't be all bad, huh? Don't mention this to the Chancellor. He doesn't approve of jelly babies. I think he's frivolous.'

THE DOCTOR, *THE INVASION OF TIME*

CRAIG: So what's the plan tonight? Pizza, booze, telly?

SOPHIE: Yeah, pizza, booze, telly.

THE LODGER

THE DOCTOR: What's for tea?

LOU: Chops. Nice couple of chops and gravy. Nothing special.

THE DOCTOR: Oh, that's special, Lou. That is so special. Chops and gravy, mmm.

PLANET OF THE DEAD

'Oh, look, they've got nibbles! I love nibbles.'

THE DOCTOR, *THE LAZARUS EXPERIMENT*

'If you're calling the butler, I'm very partial to tea and muffins.'

THE DOCTOR, *THE ANDROID INVASION*

TRYST: I am helping to conserve endangered species.

THE DOCTOR: By putting them in this machine?

TRYST: Oh, yes.

THE DOCTOR: Ah, yes, of course. Just in the same way a jam-maker conserves raspberries.

NIGHTMARE OF EDEN

DAVROS: I never waste a valuable commodity. The humanoid form makes an excellent concentrated protein. ...

THE DOCTOR: Did you bother to tell anyone they might be eating their own relatives?

DAVROS: Certainly not. That would have created what I believe is termed consumer resistance.

REVELATION OF THE DALEKS

'Why can't you give me any decent food? You're Scottish. Fry something.'

THE DOCTOR, *THE ELEVENTH HOUR*

ROSE: Oh, can you smell chips?

THE DOCTOR: Yeah. Yeah.

ROSE: Before you get me back in that box, chips it is, and you can pay.

THE DOCTOR: No money.

ROSE: What sort of date are you? Come on then, tightwad, chips are on me. We've only got five billion years till the shops close.

THE END OF THE WORLD

'If you want to know what's going on, work in the kitchens.'

THE DOCTOR, *RISE OF THE CYBERMEN*

THE DOCTOR: You know, I think it was Rassilon who once said, 'There are few ways in which a Time Lord can be more innocently occupied, than in catching fish.'

PERI: It was Dr Johnson who said that, about money.

THE TWO DOCTORS

GROSE: The Doctor said that you'd be fair famished when you woke up, so here's scrambled egg, hot buttered toast, kedgeree, kidney, sausage and bacon.

ACE: Cholesterol city.

GROSE: Oh, no dear. Perivale village.

GHOST LIGHT

THE DOCTOR: Swear to me. Swear to me on something that matters.

AMY: Fish fingers and custard.

THE DOCTOR: My life in your hands, Amelia Pond.

THE IMPOSSIBLE ASTRONAUT

SHOCKEYE: Personally I have never seen the necessity for starting a meal with a, what was your word?

THE DOCTOR: Hors d'oeuvres.

SHOCKEYE: Quite unnecessary, in my opinion. Eight or nine main dishes are quite enough…

THE TWO DOCTORS

'I think I may have accidentally invented pasta.'

THE DOCTOR, *POND LIFE*

'I think I just invented the banana daiquiri a few centuries early. Do you know, they've never even seen a banana before? Always take a banana to a party, Rose. Bananas are good.'

THE DOCTOR, *THE GIRL IN THE FIREPLACE*

'It's a floater, all right. You've got it, guv. On my oath, you wouldn't want that served with onions. Never seen anything like it in all my puff. Oh, make an 'orse sick, that would.'

GHOUL, *THE TALONS OF WENG-CHIANG*

'I've run restaurants. Who do you think invented the Yorkshire pudding? Pudding, yet savoury. Sound familiar?'

THE DOCTOR, *THE POWER OF THREE*

ROMANA: Where are we going?

THE DOCTOR: Are you talking philosophically or geographically?

ROMANA: Philosophically.

THE DOCTOR: Then we're going to lunch.

CITY OF DEATH

'Of course, in primitive times on Old Earth, they ate prodigious quantities of vegetable matter without any apparent harm to their system.'

HADE, *THE SUN MAKERS*

SHOCKEYE: Tell me, on this planet, do they ever eat their own?

THE DOCTOR: I believe in the Far Indies it has been known, but I remember a dish – shepherd's pie.

SHOCKEYE: Shepherd's pie? A shepherd? Can't we walk quicker?

THE TWO DOCTORS

THE DOCTOR: 'Throw in the apple cores very hard, put the lot in a shallow tin and bake in a high oven for two weeks.'

MRS TYLER: That ain't the way to make a fruitcake.

IMAGE OF THE FENDAHL

ARTIE: How can it be your mum's soufflé if you're making it?

CLARA: Because, Artie, it's like my mum always said. The soufflé isn't the soufflé, the soufflé is the recipe.

ANGIE: Was your mum deep on puddings?

CLARA: She was a great woman.

THE NAME OF THE DOCTOR

DORTMUN: Two more pairs of hands. Good.

DAVID: She says *she* can cook … And what do *you* do?

SUSAN: I eat.

THE DALEK INVASION OF EARTH

'Cut out the hard-boiled eggs, I said. Quite apart from their effects on my digestion, they're aesthetically boring.'

GOODGE, *TERROR OF THE AUTONS*

CLARA: OK. When are you going to explain to me what the hell is going on?

THE DOCTOR: Breakfast.

CLARA: What? I'm not waiting for breakfast.

THE DOCTOR: It's a time machine. You never have to wait for breakfast.

THE BELLS OF SAINT JOHN

'The last time I fished this particular stretch, I landed four magnificent gumblejack in less than ten minutes … The finest fish in this galaxy, probably the universe. Cleaned, skinned, quickly pan-fried in their own juices till they're golden brown. Ambrosia steeped in nectar, Peri. The flavour is unforgettable.'

THE DOCTOR, *THE TWO DOCTORS*

'Nothing like sausage sandwiches when you are working something out.'

PROFESSOR RUMFORD, *THE STONES OF BLOOD*

'Did you ever have one of those little cakes with the crunchy ball bearings on top? Do you know those things? Nobody else in this entire galaxy's ever even bothered to make edible ball bearings. Genius.'

THE DOCTOR, *FEAR HER*

SHOCKEYE: Do you serve humans here?

OSCAR: Most of the time, sir. Yes, I think I could venture to say that most of our customers are certainly human.

SHOCKEYE: I mean human meat, you fawning imbecile.

OSCAR: No, sir. The nouvelle cuisine has not yet penetrated this establishment.

THE TWO DOCTORS

'Who was it said Earthmen never invite their ancestors round to dinner?'

THE DOCTOR, *GHOST LIGHT*

'No one loves cattle more than Burger King.'

MISS KIZLET, *THE BELLS OF SAINT JOHN*

'Here, have a jelly baby and don't forget to brush your teeth.'

THE DOCTOR, *NIGHTMARE OF EDEN*

CHEERS!

'You know, one thing you can be certain of with politicians, is that whatever their political ideas, they always keep a well-stocked larder. Not to mention the cellar.'

THE DOCTOR, *DAY OF THE DALEKS*

AMY: And since when do you drink wine?

THE DOCTOR: I'm eleven hundred and three. I must've drunk it some time. Oh, why it's horrid. I thought it would taste more like the gums.

THE IMPOSSIBLE ASTRONAUT

'Patron, three glasses of water. Make them doubles.'

THE DOCTOR, *CITY OF DEATH*

ADRIC: What does that stuff taste like?

RICHARD MACE: Nectar.

ADRIC: Oh. And what does that taste like?

THE VISITATION

'Funny thing. Last time I was sentenced to death, I ordered four hyper-vodkas for my breakfast. All a bit of a blur after that. Woke up in bed with both my executioners. Mmm, lovely couple. They stayed in touch. Can't say that about most executioners.'

CAPTAIN JACK HARKNESS, *THE DOCTOR DANCES*

EMMA: Urgh. I'd rather have a nice cup of tea.

CLARA: Me too. Whisky is the eleventh most disgusting thing ever invented.

HIDE

YATES: Fancy a dance, Brigadier?

THE BRIGADIER: It's kind of you, Captain Yates. I think I'd rather have a pint.

THE DAEMONS

FANCY A BREW?

'Would you care for some tea?'

DALEK, *VICTORY OF THE DALEKS*

ZOE: There's one thing I don't understand.

MILO: Well, you're very lucky, girl. There's about a hundred thousand things I don't understand, but I don't stand around asking fool questions about them, I do something useful. Why don't you do something useful? Why don't you make us all a pot of tea or something?

THE SPACE PIRATES

BRYSON: Excuse me, sir, but are we evacuating or not?

THE BRIGADIER: No.

BRYSON: Oh, well, in that case, sir, what should I do?

THE BRIGADIER: Oh, go and make us all a cup of tea.

INVASION OF THE DINOSAURS

THE DOCTOR: Look, I said I don't want any tea today, thank you.

JO: I'm not the tea lady.

THE DOCTOR: Then what the blazes are you doing in here? … Don't you know this area is strictly out of bounds to everybody except the tea lady and the Brigadier's personal staff?

TERROR OF THE AUTONS

'The coffee's just about as filthy as UNIT tea, if that's possible.'

JO GRANT, *PLANET OF THE SPIDERS*

THE DOCTOR: I don't suppose you can make tea?

ROMANA: Tea?

THE DOCTOR: No, I don't suppose you can. They don't teach you anything useful at the Academy, do they?

THE RIBOS OPERATION

THE DOCTOR: Good. Well, now he's gone, any chance of a cup of tea?

TANE: What?!

THE DOCTOR: Or coffee. My friend and I have had a very trying experience. Haven't we had a trying experience, Harry?

HARRY: Very trying, Doctor.

TANE: Step into the security scan.

THE DOCTOR: What, no tea?

GENESIS OF THE DALEKS

CHANDLER: What be tea?

THE DOCTOR: Oh, a noxious infusion of oriental leaves containing a high percentage of toxic acid.

CHANDLER: Sounds an evil brew, don't it?

THE DOCTOR: True. Personally, I rather like it.

THE AWAKENING

BEING CHILDISH

'What's wrong with being childish? I like being childish.'

THE DOCTOR, *TERROR OF THE AUTONS*

'There's no point in being grown up if you can't be childish sometimes.'

THE DOCTOR, *ROBOT*

THE DOCTOR: Lily and Cyril's room. I'm going to be honest, masterpiece. The ultimate bedroom. A sciencey-wiencey workbench. A jungle. A maze. A window disguised as a mirror. A mirror disguised as a window. Selection of torches for midnight feasts and secret reading. Zen garden, mysterious cupboard, zone of tranquillity, rubber wall, dream tank, exact model of the rest of the house, not quite to scale. Apologies. Dolls with comical expressions, the Magna Carta, a foot spa. Cluedo! A yellow fort.

CYRIL: Where are the beds?

THE DOCTOR: Well, I couldn't fit everything in. There had to be sacrifices. Anyway, who needs beds when you've got hammocks!

THE DOCTOR, THE WIDOW AND THE WARDROBE

'It goes up tiddly up, it goes down tiddly down for only £49.99, which I personally think is a bit steep, but then again it's your parents' cash and they'll only waste it on boring stuff like lamps and vegetables. Yawn.'

THE DOCTOR, *CLOSING TIME*

'I expect chocolate for breakfast. If you don't feel sick by mid-morning you're not doing it right.'

THE GANGER DOCTOR, *THE ALMOST PEOPLE*

THE DOCTOR: Right then, your bedroom. Great. Let's see. You're twelve years old, so we'll stay away from under the bed. Cupboard! Big cupboard. I love a cupboard. Do you know, there's a thing called a face spider. It's just like a tiny baby's head with spider legs, and it's specifically evolved to scuttle up the backs of bedroom cupboards... which, yeah, I probably shouldn't have mentioned. Right. So. What are we going to do? Eat crisps and talk about girls? I've never actually done that, but I bet it's easy. Girls? Yeah?

KAZRAN: Are you really a babysitter?

THE DOCTOR: I think you'll find I'm universally recognised as a mature and responsible adult.

A CHRISTMAS CAROL

'I know you can't wrap your hand around your elbow and make your fingers meet.'

THE DOCTOR, *THE IDIOT'S LANTERN*

'That is the dematerialising control and that, over yonder, is the horizontal hold. Up there is the scanner, those are the doors, that is a chair with a panda on it. Sheer poetry, dear boy. Now please stop bothering me.'

THE DOCTOR, *THE TIME MEDDLER*

'Never knowingly be serious. Rule 27. You might want to write these down.'

THE DOCTOR, *LET'S KILL HITLER*

'Do you have to talk like children? What is it that makes you so ashamed of being a grown-up?'

THE WAR DOCTOR, *THE DAY OF THE DOCTOR*

CHRISTMAS

'A Happy Christmas to all of you at home.'

THE DOCTOR, *THE DALEKS' MASTER PLAN*

'What sort of man doesn't carry a trowel? Put it on your Christmas list.'

BRIAN, *DINOSAURS ON A SPACESHIP*

'Christmas Eve on a rooftop. Saw a chimney, my whole brain just went, what the hell.'

THE DOCTOR, *A CHRISTMAS CAROL*

LINDA: How's the turkey doing?

CLARA: Great. Yeah, yeah, it's doing great. Well, dead and decapitated, but that's Christmas when you're a turkey.

THE TIME OF THE DOCTOR

IDA: Well, we've come this far. There's no turning back.

THE DOCTOR: Oh, did you have to? No turning back? That's almost as bad as nothing can possibly go wrong, or this is going to be the best Christmas Walford's ever had.

THE IMPOSSIBLE PLANET

THE DOCTOR: Father Christmas, Santa Claus or, as I've always known him, Jeff.

BOY: There's no such person as Father Christmas.

THE DOCTOR: Oh, yeah? Me and Father Christmas, Frank Sinatra's hunting lodge, 1952. See him at the back with the blonde? Albert Einstein. The three of us together. Brr. Watch out. OK? Keep the faith. Stay off the naughty list.

A CHRISTMAS CAROL

'It was a present, and it wasn't supposed to be opened till Christmas Day. Honestly, who opens their Christmas presents early? OK. Shut up. Everyone.'

THE DOCTOR, *THE DOCTOR, THE WIDOW AND THE WARDROBE*

AMY: We're about to have Christmas dinner. Joining us?

THE DOCTOR: If it's no trouble.

RORY: There's a place set for you.

THE DOCTOR: But you didn't know I was coming. Why would you set me a place?

AMY: Oh, because we always do. It's Christmas, you moron.

THE DOCTOR, THE WIDOW AND THE WARDROBE

'Back to your mum. It's all waiting. Fish and chips, sausage and mash, beans on toast... no, Christmas! Turkey! Although, having met your mother, nut loaf would be more appropriate.'

THE DOCTOR, *BORN AGAIN*

'That's human Christmas out there! They eat so much. All that roasting meat, cakes and red wine. Hot fat blood food. Pots and plates of meat and flesh … and grease and juice. And baking burnt sticky hot skin. Hot, it's so hot!'

THE MASTER, *THE END OF TIME*

'On every world, wherever people are, in the deepest part of the winter, at the exact mid-point, everybody stops and turns and hugs, as if to say, well done. Well done, everyone. We're halfway out of the dark. Back on Earth, we called this Christmas, or the Winter Solstice. On this world, the first settlers called it the Crystal Feast. You know what I call it? I call it expecting something for nothing.'

KAZRAN SARDICK, *A CHRISTMAS CAROL*

MADGE: No one should be alone at Christmas.

THE DOCTOR: I'm fine. I don't mind. I'm really very good at being—

MADGE: I'm not talking about you, I'm talking about your friends. You can't let them think that you're dead. Not at Christmas.

THE DOCTOR, THE WIDOW AND THE WARDROBE

SARDICK: I despise Christmas.

THE DOCTOR: You shouldn't. It's very you.

SARDICK: It's what? What do you mean?

THE DOCTOR: Halfway out of the dark.

A CHRISTMAS CAROL

'Santa's a robot!'

DONNA, *THE RUNAWAY BRIDE*

'I am Mr Copper, the ship's historian, and I shall be taking you to Old London Town in the country of Yookay. Ruled over by Good King Wenceslas. Now human beings worshipped the great god Santa, a creature with fearsome claws, and his wife Mary. And every Christmas Eve, the people of Yookay go to war with the country of Turkey. They then eat the Turkey people for Christmas dinner. Like savages.'

MR COPPER, *VOYAGE OF THE DAMNED*

MR COPPER: Rather ironic, but this is very much in the spirit of Christmas. It's a festival of violence. They say that human beings only survive depending on whether they've been good or bad. It's barbaric!

THE DOCTOR: Actually, that's not true. Christmas is a time of peace and thanksgiving and – What am I going on about? My Christmasses are always like this.

VOYAGE OF THE DAMNED

Chapter Eight:
The Past

'This is what I travel for, Rose.
To see history happening
right in front of us.'

THE DOCTOR, *ALIENS OF LONDON*

FIXED POINTS IN TIME

'But you can't rewrite history! Not one line!'

THE DOCTOR, *THE AZTECS*

'The events will happen, just as they are written. I'm afraid so and we can't stem the tide. But at least we can stop being carried away with the flood!'

THE DOCTOR, *THE REIGN OF TERROR*

'Crossing into established events is strictly forbidden. Except for cheap tricks.'

THE DOCTOR, *SMITH AND JONES*

THE DOCTOR: Are you quite mad? You know as well as I do the golden rule about space and time travelling. Never, never interfere with the course of history.

MONK: And who says so? Doctor, it's more fun my way. I can make things happen ahead of their time.

THE TIME MEDDLER

'Rose, there's a man alive in the world who wasn't alive before. An ordinary man. That's the most important thing in creation. The whole world's different because he's alive.'

THE DOCTOR, *FATHER'S DAY*

'Now listen to me, both of you. There are some rules that cannot be broken even with the TARDIS. Don't ever ask me to do anything like that again. You must accept that Adric is dead. His life wasn't wasted. He died trying to save others, just like his brother, Varsh. You know, Adric had a choice. This is the way he wanted it.'

THE DOCTOR, *TIME-FLIGHT*

'My dear Steven, history sometimes gives us a terrible shock, and that is because we don't quite fully understand. Why should we? After all, we're all too small to realise its final pattern. Therefore don't try and judge it from where you stand. I was right to do as I did. Yes, that I firmly believe.'

THE DOCTOR, *THE MASSACRE*

'This moment, this precise moment in time, it's like… I mean, it's only a theory, what do I know, but I think certain moments in time are fixed. Tiny, precious moments. Everything else is in flux, anything can happen, but those certain moments, they have to stand. This base on Mars with you, Adelaide Brooke, this is one vital moment. What happens here must always happen.'

THE DOCTOR, *THE WATERS OF MARS*

AMY: But it could help us find Rory.

THE DOCTOR: And if you read ahead and find that Rory dies? This isn't any old future, Amy, it's ours. Once we know what's coming, it's fixed. I'm going to break something, because you told me that I'm going to do it. No choice now.

AMY: Time can be rewritten.

THE DOCTOR: Not once you've read it. Once we know what's coming, it's written in stone.

THE ANGELS TAKE MANHATTAN

STEPPING INTO THE PAST

'You may know where you are, my dears, but not when. Oh, I can foresee oodles of trouble.'

THE DOCTOR, *THE SMUGGLERS*

THE DOCTOR: Three o'clock, June the 11th, 1925.

TEGAN: I haven't been born yet.

THE DOCTOR: It's interesting, isn't it? And no jet lag.

BLACK ORCHID

'Time isn't a straight line. It's all bumpy-wumpy. There's loads of boring stuff like Sundays and Tuesdays and Thursday afternoons. But now and then there are Saturdays. Big temporal tipping points when anything's possible. The TARDIS can't resist them, like a moth to a flame. She loves a party, so I give her 1969 and NASA, because that's space in the Sixties, and Canton Everett Delaware III, and this is where she's pointing.'

THE DOCTOR, *THE IMPOSSIBLE ASTRONAUT*

ROSE: It's so weird. The day my father died. I thought it'd be all sort of grim and stormy. It's just an ordinary day.

THE DOCTOR: The past is another country. 1987's just the Isle of Wight.

FATHER'S DAY

'The point of archaeology is to carefully recover the past, not disintegrate it.'

THE DOCTOR, *BATTLEFIELD*

MARTHA: I'm not going to get carted off as a slave, am I?

THE DOCTOR: Why would they do that?

MARTHA: Not exactly white, in case you haven't noticed.

THE DOCTOR: I'm not even human. Just walk about like you own the place. Works for me.

THE SHAKESPEARE CODE

BILLY: Where am I?

THE DOCTOR: 1969. Not bad, as it goes. You've got the moon landing to look forward to.

MARTHA: Oh, the moon landing's brilliant. We went four times.

BLINK

'Roll back time, I see. Can Whitaker really do that? … Do you realise what'll happen if they succeed? … There never was a golden age, Mike. It's all an illusion.'

THE DOCTOR, *INVASION OF THE DINOSAURS*

'Don't mess with Egyptian queens.'

THE DOCTOR, *DINOSAURS ON A SPACESHIP*

'Definitely Jurassic. There's a nip in the air, though. We can't be far off the Pleistocene era… It's times like this I wish I still had my scarf. Better watch out for the odd brontosaurus.'

THE DOCTOR, *TIME-FLIGHT*

LYNDA: A hundred years ago? What, you were here a hundred years ago?

THE DOCTOR: Yep!

LYNDA: You're looking good on it.

THE DOCTOR: I moisturise.

BAD WOLF

THE DOCTOR: I'm a time traveller. Or I was. I'm stuck in 1969.

MARTHA: We're stuck. All of space and time, he promised me. Now I've got a job in a shop. I've got to support him!

BLINK

SCARLIONI: Doctor, how very nice to see you again. It seems like only 474 years since we last met.

THE DOCTOR: Indeed, indeed, yes. I so much prefer the weather in the early part of the sixteenth century, don't you?

CITY OF DEATH

YOUNG REINETTE: Monsieur, what are you doing in my fireplace?

THE DOCTOR: Oh, it's just a routine fire check. Can you tell me what year it is?

YOUNG REINETTE: Of course I can. Seventeen hundred and twenty-seven.

THE DOCTOR: Right, lovely. One of my favourites. August is rubbish though. Stay indoors. OK, that's all for now. Thanks for your help. Hope you enjoy the rest of the fire. Night, night.

THE GIRL IN THE FIREPLACE

THE DOCTOR: Oh, smell that air. Grass and lemonade. And a little bit of mint. A hint of mint. Must be the 1920s.

DONNA: You can tell what year it is just by smelling?

THE DOCTOR: Oh, yeah.

DONNA: Or maybe that big vintage car coming up the drive gave it away.

THE UNICORN AND THE WASP

'Oh, the Lake District's lovely. Let's definitely go there. We can eat scones. They do great scones in 1927.'

THE DOCTOR, *THE RINGS OF AKHATEN*

'1979. Hell of a year. China invades Vietnam. *The Muppet Movie*. Love that film. Margaret Thatcher. Urgh. Skylab falls to Earth, with a little help from me. Nearly took off my thumb.'

THE DOCTOR, *TOOTH AND CLAW*

THE DOCTOR: A chemical reaction in a primeval swamp can create life on a planet. Why couldn't the universe be created by a similar chance factor, hmm?

KARI: But exploding fuel in space? It's almost too simple.

THE DOCTOR: It only appears simple because the circumstances were exactly right.

TERMINUS

JAMIE: Ach, here's you saying you're a doctor, you've not even bled him yet.

BEN: What's he on about?

THE DOCTOR: Bloodletting.

BEN: Yeah, but that's stupid.

JAMIE: It's the only way of curing the sick.

BEN: Killing him, more like.

THE HIGHLANDERS

TEGAN: 1851. The Great Exhibition?

THE DOCTOR: All the wonders of Victorian science and technology.

TEGAN: Well, the TARDIS should feel at home.

TIME-FLIGHT

THE DOCTOR: A monastery. Thirteenth century.

AMY: Oh, we've gone all medieval.

RORY: I'm not sure about that.

AMY: Really? Medieval expert are you?

RORY: No, it's just that I can hear Dusty Springfield.

THE REBEL FLESH

THE DOCTOR: I had this friend, once. She called me spaceman.

CHRISTINA: And was she right? Do you zoom about the place in a rocket?

THE DOCTOR: Well, a little blue box. Travels in more than space. It can journey through time, Christina. Oh, the places I've been. World War One. Creation of the universe. End of the universe. The war between China and Japan. And the Court of King Athelstan in 924 AD.

PLANET OF THE DEAD

THE DOCTOR: The Blitz.

LAZARUS: You've read about it.

THE DOCTOR: I was there.

LAZARUS: You're too young.

THE DOCTOR: So are you.

THE LAZARUS EXPERIMENT

CRAIG: Oh, that was incredible. That was absolutely brilliant. Where did you learn to cook?

THE DOCTOR: Paris, in the eighteenth century. No, hang on, that's not recent, is it? Seventeenth? No, no, no. Twentieth. Sorry, I'm not used to doing them in the right order.

THE LODGER

THE DOCTOR: What Paris has, it has an ethos, a life. It has...

ROMANA: A bouquet?

THE DOCTOR: A spirit all of its own. Like a wine, it has...

ROMANA: A bouquet.

THE DOCTOR: It has a bouquet. Yes. Like a good wine. You have to choose one of the vintage years, of course.

ROMANA: What year is this?

THE DOCTOR: Ah well, yes. It's 1979 actually. More of a table wine, shall we say.

CITY OF DEATH

LEELA: In a house this size there must be protection. The professor will have weapons in fixed positions to guard the approaches.

THE DOCTOR: I brought you to the wrong time, my girl. You'd have loved Agincourt.

THE TALONS OF WENG-CHIANG

'Look, sorry, I've got a bit of a complex life. Things don't always happen to me in quite the right order. Gets a bit confusing at times, especially at weddings. I'm rubbish at weddings, especially my own.'

THE DOCTOR, *BLINK*

MICKEY: What's a horse doing on a spaceship?

THE DOCTOR: Mickey, what's pre-Revolutionary France doing on a spaceship? Get a little perspective.

THE GIRL IN THE FIREPLACE

ROMANA: Well, there's one called Zolfa-Thura. That's in the history books.

THE DOCTOR: Well, they're all in somebody's history books.

MEGLOS

NAME DROPPER

GRACE: You know, Freud had a name for that.

THE MASTER: Transference.

THE DOCTOR: Yes, very witty, Grace. At least Freud would have taken me seriously.

GRACE: He'd have hung up his pipe if he'd met you.

THE DOCTOR: Actually, we did meet.

GRACE: Oh, that's right. He's a Time Lord.

THE DOCTOR: We got on very well.

DOCTOR WHO (TV MOVIE)

'Look after this. I love that coat. Janis Joplin gave me that coat.'

THE DOCTOR, *GRIDLOCK*

THE DOCTOR: You know, I haven't seen a coronation since Elizabeth I's. Or was it Queen Victoria?

JO: Name dropper.

THE CURSE OF PELADON

THE DOCTOR: If Horatio Nelson had been in charge of this operation, I hardly think that he would have waited for official instructions.

CAPTAIN HART: Yes... a pretty impulsive fellow. If one can believe the history books.

THE DOCTOR: History books? Captain Hart, Horatio Nelson was a personal friend of mine.

THE SEA DEVILS

'I was on board another ship once. They said that was unsinkable. I ended up clinging to an iceberg. It wasn't half cold.'

THE DOCTOR, *THE END OF THE WORLD*

MORGAN: Something you want, sir?

THE DOCTOR: Yes. A telephone that works. Yours is out of order.

MORGAN: Likely it is.

THE DOCTOR: So is the village call box.

MORGAN: There was a gale last night, sir. Brought all the lines down.

THE DOCTOR: Ah. I always told Alexander Bell that wires were unreliable.

THE ANDROID INVASION

THE DOCTOR: The sun's gone wibbly, so right now, somewhere out there, there's going to be a big old video conference call. All the experts in the world panicking at once, and do you know what they need? Me. Ah, and here they all are. All the big boys. NASA, Jodrell Bank, Tokyo Space Centre, Patrick Moore.

MRS ANGELO: I like Patrick Moore.

THE DOCTOR: I'll get you his number. But watch him, he's a devil.

THE ELEVENTH HOUR

'All I care about is getting back to the TARDIS, where it's nice and warm. No wonder they forced him to sign Magna Carta. Bet there was something in it about underheated housing.'

TEGAN, *THE KING'S DEMONS*

'Agatha Christie. I was just talking about you the other day. I said, I bet she's brilliant. I'm the Doctor. This is Donna. Oh, I love your stuff. What a mind. You fool me every time. Well, almost every time. Well, once or twice. Well, once. But it was a good once.'

THE DOCTOR, *THE UNICORN AND THE WASP*

THE DOCTOR: Attaboy, Charlie.

CHARLES DICKENS: Nobody calls me Charlie.

THE DOCTOR: The ladies do.

THE UNQUIET DEAD

DONNA: No, but isn't that a bit weird? Agatha Christie didn't walk around surrounded by murders. Not really. I mean, that's like meeting Charles Dickens and he's surrounded by ghosts at Christmas.

THE DOCTOR: Well…

DONNA: Oh, come on! It's not like we could drive across country and find Enid Blyton having tea with Noddy. Could we? Noddy's not real. Is he? Tell me there's no Noddy.

THE DOCTOR: There's no Noddy.

THE UNICORN AND THE WASP

SARAH: It's probably been vandalised.

THE DOCTOR: That's a very unfair word, you know, because actually the Vandals were quite decent chaps.

INVASION OF THE DINOSAURS

CORDO: Each Megropolis was given its own sun.

THE DOCTOR: In-station fusion satellites. Galileo would have been impressed.

THE SUN MAKERS

SARAH: Oh, it's no good, Doctor. They won't budge.

THE DOCTOR: Hmm? I used a tangle Turk's Head eye-splice with a gromit I picked up from Houdini. It should work.

REVENGE OF THE CYBERMEN

LEELA: Where did you learn to shoot like that?

THE DOCTOR: Shoot like what? Oh, like that. In Switzerland. Charming man. William Tell, he was called.

THE FACE OF EVIL

STOKER: It's only to be expected. There's a thunderstorm moving in and lightning is a form of static electricity, as was first proven by... Anyone?

THE DOCTOR: Benjamin Franklin.

STOKER: Correct.

THE DOCTOR: My mate, Ben. That was a day and a half. I got rope burns off that kite, and then I got soaked.

STOKER: Quite.

THE DOCTOR: And then I got electrocuted.

SMITH AND JONES

MARTHA: I didn't know you could play?

THE DOCTOR: Oh, well, you know, if you hang around with Beethoven, you're bound to pick a few things up.

THE LAZARUS EXPERIMENT

'I'm telling you. Lloyd George, he used to drink me under the table.'

THE DOCTOR, *ALIENS OF LONDON*

'French picklock. Never fails. Belonged to Marie Antoinette. Charming lady. Lost her head, poor thing.'

THE DOCTOR, *PYRAMIDS OF MARS*

ROMANA: Newton. Who's Newton?

THE DOCTOR: Old Isaac? Friend of mine on Earth. Discovered gravity. Well, I say he discovered gravity. I had to give him a bit of a prod.

ROMANA: What did you do?

THE DOCTOR: Climbed up a tree.

ROMANA: And?

THE DOCTOR: Dropped an apple on his head.

ROMANA: Ah. And so he discovered gravity?

THE DOCTOR: No, no. He told me to clear off out of his tree. I explained it to him afterwards at dinner.

THE PIRATE PLANET

'Pity about the scarf. Madame Nostradamus made it for me. A witty little knitter... Never get another one like it.'

THE DOCTOR, *THE ARK IN SPACE*

THE DOCTOR: I met him once, you know.

SARAH: Who?

THE DOCTOR: Shakespeare. Charming fellow. Dreadful actor.

SARAH: Perhaps that's why he took up writing.

THE DOCTOR: Perhaps it was.

PLANET OF EVIL

COUNTESS: *Hamlet*. The first draft.

THE DOCTOR: What? It's been missing for centuries.

COUNTESS: It's quite genuine, I assure you.

THE DOCTOR: I know. I recognise the handwriting.

COUNTESS: Shakespeare's.

THE DOCTOR: No, mine. He'd sprained his wrist writing sonnets. Wonderful stuff. 'To be or not to be, that is the question. Whether 'tis nobler in the mind to suffer the slings and arrows of outrageous fortune or to take arms against a sea of troubles and...' 'Take arms against a sea of troubles'? That's a mixed... I told him that was a mixed metaphor and he would insist.

CITY OF DEATH

THE DOCTOR: Come on. We can all have a good flirt later.

SHAKESPEARE: Is that a promise, Doctor?

THE DOCTOR: Oh, fifty-seven academics just punched the air.

THE SHAKESPEARE CODE

'Trust yourself. When you're locked away in your room, the words just come, don't they, like magic. Words of the right sound, the right shape, the right rhythm. Words that last for ever. That's what you do, Will. You choose perfect words. Do it. Improvise.'

THE DOCTOR TO WILLIAM SHAKESPEARE, *THE SHAKESPEARE CODE*

'Perhaps it is time we were leaving. We don't want to be blamed for starting a fire, do we? … I had enough of that in 1666.'

THE DOCTOR, *PYRAMIDS OF MARS*

'And Picasso. What a ghastly old goat. I kept telling him, "Concentrate, Pablo. It's one eye, either side of the face."'

THE DOCTOR, *VINCENT AND THE DOCTOR*

ROMANA: 'To the Doctor. A souvenir with love and thanks for all his help with the Minotaur. Theseus and Ariadne.'

THE DOCTOR: Yes. If I hadn't produced that ball of string to find a way out of the labyrinth, they were going to unravel my scarf, the wretches.

THE CREATURE FROM THE PIT

'I remember watching Michelangelo painting the Sistine Chapel. Wow! What a whinger. I kept saying to him, look, if you're scared of heights, you shouldn't have taken the job, then.'

THE DOCTOR, *VINCENT AND THE DOCTOR*

THE DOCTOR: Poisson? Reinette Poisson? No! No, no, no, no, no way. Reinette Poisson? Later Madame Étoiles? Later still mistress of Louis XV, uncrowned Queen of France? Actress, artist, musician, dancer, courtesan, fantastic gardener!

SERVANT: Who the hell are you?!

THE DOCTOR: I'm the Doctor, and I just snogged Madame de Pompadour.

THE GIRL IN THE FIREPLACE

THE DOCTOR: Oh, it doesn't work like that, Winston, and it's going to be tough. There are terrible days to come. The darkest days. But you can do it. You know you can.

CHURCHILL: Stay with us, and help us win through. The world needs you.

THE DOCTOR: The world doesn't need me.

CHURCHILL: No?

THE DOCTOR: The world's got Winston Spencer Churchill.

VICTORY OF THE DALEKS

THE DOCTOR: Rory, take Hitler and put him in that cupboard over there. Now, do it.

RORY: Right. Putting Hitler in the cupboard. Cupboard, Hitler. Hitler, cupboard. Come on.

LET'S KILL HITLER

GRACE: Did you know Madame Curie, too?

THE DOCTOR: Intimately.

GRACE: Did she kiss as good as me?

THE MASTER: As *well* as you.

DOCTOR WHO (TV MOVIE)

'I can't tell the future,
I just work there.'

THE DOCTOR, *THE BELLS OF SAINT JOHN*

DAYS TO COME

'Every great decision creates ripples, like a huge boulder dropped in a lake. The ripples merge, rebound off the banks in unforeseeable ways. The heavier the decision, the larger the waves, the more uncertain the consequences.'

THE DOCTOR, *REMEMBRANCE OF THE DALEKS*

'Highness, it is not well to think of the past, there is still the future to make.'

SHOLAKH, *THE RIBOS OPERATION*

DODO: Doctor, do you think we'll ever see him again?

THE DOCTOR: Well, who knows, my dear? In this strange complex of time and space, anything can happen. Come along, little one. We must go. We mustn't look back.

THE SAVAGES

THE DOCTOR: Our lives are important, at least to us. But as we see, so we learn.

IAN: And what are we going to see and learn next, Doctor?

THE DOCTOR: Well, unlike the old adage, my boy, our destiny is in the stars, so let's go and search for it.

THE REIGN OF TERROR

'Hello, Stormageddon. It's the Doctor. Here to help. Shush. Hey. There, there. Be quiet. Go to sleep. Really. Stop crying. You've got a lot to look forward to, you know. A normal human life on Earth. Mortgage repayments, the nine to five, a persistent nagging sense of spiritual emptiness. Save the tears for later, boy-o. Oh, no. That was crabby. No, that was old. But I am old, Stormy. I am so old. So near the end. You, Alfie Owens, you are so young, aren't you? And, you know, right now, everything's ahead of you. You could be anything. Yes, I know. You could walk among the stars. They don't actually look like that, you know. They are rather more impressive. Yeah. You know, when I was little like you, I dreamt of the stars. I think it's fair to say in the language of your age, that I lived my dream, I owned the stage, gave it a hundred and ten per cent. I hope you have as much fun as I did, Alfie.'

THE DOCTOR, *CLOSING TIME*

'You lot, you spend all your time thinking about dying, like you're going to get killed by eggs or beef or global warming or asteroids. But you never take time to imagine the impossible, that maybe you survive. This is the year five point five slash apple slash twenty-six. Five billion years in your future, and this is the day... Hold on... This is the day the sun expands. Welcome to the end of the world.'

THE DOCTOR, *THE END OF THE WORLD*

'So maybe this is it. First contact. The day mankind officially comes into contact with an alien race. I'm not interfering because you've got to handle this on your own. That's when the human race finally grows up. Just this morning you were all tiny and small and made of clay. Now you can expand.'

THE DOCTOR, *ALIENS OF LONDON*

'There are fixed points through time where things must always stay the way they are. This is not one of them. This is an opportunity. A temporal tipping point. Whatever happens today will change future events, create its own timeline, its own reality. The future pivots around you, here, now. So do good, for humanity, and for Earth.'

THE DOCTOR, *COLD BLOOD*

'People assume that time is a strict progression of cause to effect, but actually from a non-linear, non-subjective viewpoint, it's more like a big ball of wibbly-wobbly, timey-wimey stuff.'

THE DOCTOR, *BLINK*

DESTINY

'Time will tell. It always does.'

THE DOCTOR, *REMEMBRANCE OF THE DALEKS*

'Destiny. Isn't that just a fancy name for blind chance?'

PERI, *THE TRIAL OF A TIME LORD: MINDWARP*

'When faced with the inevitable, don't waste precious time by resisting it.'

THE DOCTOR, *PLANET OF THE DALEKS*

THE DOCTOR: Sometimes knowing your own future's what enables you to change it. Especially if you're bloody-minded, contradictory, and completely unpredictable.

RORY: So basically, if you're Amy, then?

THE DOCTOR: Yes, if anyone could defeat pre-destiny, it's your wife.

THE GIRL WHO WAITED

'You wanted advice, you said. I never give it. Never. But I might just say this to you. Always search for truth. My truth is in the stars and yours is here.'

THE DOCTOR, *THE DALEKS*

'Never mind the mights, my dear, just concentrate on what you're doing.'

THE DOCTOR, *THE CRUSADE*

DAVROS: Do you believe your puny efforts can change the course of destiny?

THE DOCTOR: Well, let's just say I might tamper with it.

DESTINY OF THE DALEKS

'I've never struggled against the inevitable. It's a vain occupation. But I should always advise you to examine very closely what you think to be inevitable. It's surprising how often apparent defeat can be turned to victory.'

TEMMOSUS, *THE DALEKS*

'The universe hangs by such a delicate thread of coincidences. It's useless to meddle with it, unless, like me, you're a Time Lord.'

THE DOCTOR, *DOCTOR WHO* (TV MOVIE)

'There's no such thing as foretelling. Trust a time traveller.'

THE DOCTOR, *THE DOCTOR, THE WIDOW AND THE WARDROBE*

HOPE AND OPTIMISM

'Nothing in the world can stop me now!'

ZAROFF, *THE UNDERWATER MENACE*

'Sit down and write out the menus. First course interrupted by bomb explosion. Second course affected by earthquakes. Third course ruined by interference in the kitchen. I'm going out for a walk. It'll probably rain.'

GRIFFIN, *THE ENEMY OF THE WORLD*

ROMANA: There must be a huge nuclear war going on down there.

THE DOCTOR: Not at all, no.

ROMANA: What else could it be.

THE DOCTOR: I don't know. Probably someone giving a huge breakfast party … Why do you always assume the worst?

ROMANA: Because it usually happens.

THE DOCTOR: Empirical poppycock! Where's your joy in life? Where's your optimism?

ROMANA: It opted out.

THE ARMAGEDDON FACTOR

'Have you ever thought what it's like to be wanderers in the fourth dimension? Have you? To be exiles? Susan and I are cut off from our own planet, without friends or protection. But one day we shall get back. Yes, one day. One day.'

THE DOCTOR, *AN UNEARTHLY CHILD*

'You must travel with understanding as well as hope.'

THE DOCTOR, *THE ARK*

'Nil desperandum, Jo.'

THE DOCTOR, *THE GREEN DEATH*

'No one knows how they're going to be remembered. All we can do is hope for the best.'

THE DOCTOR, *THE UNICORN AND THE WASP*

THE DOCTOR: I don't know, but every single instinct of mine is telling me to get off this planet right now.

CHRISTINA: And do you think we can?

THE DOCTOR: I live in hope.

CHRISTINA: That must be nice.

PLANET OF THE DEAD

'You see, I know that although the Daleks will create havoc and destruction for millions of years, I know also that out of their evil must come something good.'

THE DOCTOR, *GENESIS OF THE DALEKS*

ROMANA: How did you know?

THE DOCTOR: Oh, knowing's easy. Everyone does that ad nauseam. I just sort of hope.

STATE OF DECAY

'Any hope is better than none.'

IAN, *AN UNEARTHLY CHILD*

'When I was a little boy, we used to live in a house that was perched halfway up the top of a mountain. And behind our house, there sat under a tree an old man, a hermit, a monk. He'd lived under this tree for half his lifetime, so they said, and he'd learned the secret of life. So, when my black day came, I went and asked him to help me … I'll never forget what it was like up there. All bleak and cold, it was. A few bare rocks with some weeds sprouting from them and some pathetic little patches of sludgy snow. It was just grey. Grey, grey, grey. Well, the tree the old man sat under, that was ancient and twisted and the old man himself was, he was as brittle and as dry as a leaf in the autumn … He just sat there, silently, expressionless, and he listened whilst I poured out my troubles to him. I was too unhappy even for tears, I remember. And when I'd finished, he lifted a skeletal hand and he pointed. Do you know what he pointed at? … A flower. One of those little weeds. Just like a daisy, it was. Well, I looked at it for a moment and suddenly I saw it through his eyes. It was simply glowing with life, like a perfectly cut jewel. And the colours? Well, the colours were deeper and richer than anything you could possibly imagine. Yes, that was the daisiest daisy I'd ever seen … I got up and I ran down that mountain and I found that the rocks weren't grey at all, but they were red, brown and purple and gold. And those pathetic little patches of sludgy snow, they were shining white. Shining white in the sunlight.'

THE DOCTOR, *THE TIME MONSTER*

THE DOCTOR: Nothing's impossible. There's always an answer if you can find it.

JO: Yeah, such as?

THE DOCTOR: Well, that's the trouble, finding it.

CARNIVAL OF MONSTERS

'It's never too late, as a wise person once said. Kylie, I think.'

THE DOCTOR, *THE IDIOT'S LANTERN*

LITTLE SEEMS TO HAVE CHANGED

LOGIN: A little patience goes a long way.

THE DOCTOR: Yes. Too much patience goes absolutely nowhere.

FULL CIRCLE

JUDSON: Oh yes, the machine can do it. This is the first. In the future there'll be many more computing machines, thinking machines.

MILLINGTON: Yes, but whose thoughts will they think?

THE CURSE OF FENRIC

TEGAN: What year are we in?

THE DOCTOR: Around 2084.

TEGAN: Little seems to have changed since my time.

THE DOCTOR: Absolutely nothing, Tegan. There are still two power blocs, fingers poised to annihilate each other.

WARRIORS OF THE DEEP

'If it is a disease, what has caused it? Once we were farmers and hunters. The land was green, the rivers ran clear, the air was sweet to breathe. And then the Overlords came, bringing Earth's poisons with them, calling it progress. We toiled in their mines, we became slaves. Worse than slaves!'

KY, *THE MUTANTS*

'Well, the Earth these people know now, Jo, in the thirtieth-century empire, is even more grey and misty ... Land and sea alike, all grey. Grey cities linked by grey highways across grey deserts ... Slag, ash, clinker. The fruits of technology.'

THE DOCTOR, *THE MUTANTS*

'Veruna is where one of the last surviving groups of mankind took shelter in the great, er... Yes. Well, I suppose you've got all that to look forward to, haven't you.'

THE DOCTOR, *FRONTIOS*

'Wheel turns, civilisations arise, wheel turns, civilisations fall.'

PANNA, *KINDA*

DONNA: 4126? It's 4126. I'm in 4126.

THE DOCTOR: It's good, isn't it?

DONNA: What's the Earth like now?

THE DOCTOR: Bit full. But you see, the Empire stretches out across three galaxies.

DONNA: It's weird. I mean, it's brilliant, but... Back home, the papers and the telly, they keep saying we haven't got long to live. Global warming, flooding, all the bees disappearing...

THE DOCTOR: Yeah. That thing about the bees is odd.

DONNA: But look at us. We're everywhere. Is that good or bad, though? I mean, are we like explorers? Or more like a virus?

THE DOCTOR: Sometimes I wonder.

PLANET OF THE OOD

ARAK: No more executions, torture, nothing.

ETTA: It's all changed. We're free.

ARAK: Are we?

ETTA: Yes.

ARAK: What shall we do?

ETTA: Dunno.

VENGEANCE ON VAROS

THE BEST LAID PLANS

THE BRIGADIER: It's pretty hard to keep an eye on all these scientist chaps at home, so I had these cubicles put up on several floors. Confined the whole lot to barracks. All my eggs in one basket, so to speak.

THE DOCTOR: That's fine, so long as no one steals the basket.

THE TIME WARRIOR

'You know how it is. You put things off for a day, next thing you know it's a hundred years later.'

THE DOCTOR, *ARC OF INFINITY*

THE DOCTOR: A quarter of a mile straight ahead, and from there we're going to stabilise the wreckage, stop the Angels, and cure Amy.

RIVER: How?

THE DOCTOR: I'll do a thing.

RIVER: What thing?

THE DOCTOR: I don't know. It's a thing in progress. Respect the thing.

FLESH AND STONE

GROWING OLD

JO: How does it work?

THE DOCTOR: Anti-magnetic cohesion, I should think.

JO: Never heard of it.

THE DOCTOR: No, you wouldn't have done, Jo. You were born about a thousand years too early for that.

JO: Oh, I do love being with you, Doctor. You make me feel so young.

CARNIVAL OF MONSTERS

KHAN: Oh, what a trial old age is.

THE DOCTOR: It must be borne with dignity, sir.

MARCO POLO

'I'm old enough to know that a longer life isn't always a better one. In the end, you just get tired. Tired of the struggle, tired of losing everyone that matters to you, tired of watching everything turn to dust. If you live long enough, Lazarus, the only certainty left is that you'll end up alone.'

THE DOCTOR, *THE LAZARUS EXPERIMENT*

'There's no doubt about it, all this rushing around takes it out of you – particularly when you're 1250 years old.'

THE DOCTOR, *THE LEISURE HIVE*

ENDINGS

'The universe has to move forward. Pain and loss, they define us as much as happiness or love. Whether it's a world, or a relationship, everything has its time. And everything ends.'

SARAH, *SCHOOL REUNION*

'Everything has its time and everything dies.'

THE DOCTOR, *THE END OF THE WORLD*

EMMA: What's wrong?

CLARA: I just saw something I wish I hadn't.

EMMA: What did you see?

CLARA: That everything ends.

EMMA: No, not everything. Not love. Not always.

HIDE

'Never let him see the damage. And never, ever let him see you age. He doesn't like endings.'

RIVER SONG, *THE ANGELS TAKE MANHATTAN*

'Why aren't there any lights? I miss lights. You don't really miss things till they're gone, do you? It's like what my nan used to say. You'll never miss the water till the well runs dry.'

RORY, *NIGHT TERRORS*

'My Aunt Vanessa said, when I became an air stewardess, if you stop enjoying it, give it up.'

TEGAN, *RESURRECTION OF THE DALEKS*

'End the day with a smile.'

COLBY, *IMAGE OF THE FENDAHL*

'Time Lord, last of. Heard of them? Legend or anything? Not even a myth? Blimey, end of the universe is a bit humbling.'

THE DOCTOR, *UTOPIA*

'Day I know everything? Might as well stop.'

THE DOCTOR, *THE SATAN PIT*

FAREWELLS

'It's hard to leave when you haven't said goodbye.'

RIVER SONG, *THE NAME OF THE DOCTOR*

'Even after all this time he cannot understand. I dare not change the course of history. Well, at least I taught him to take some precautions. He did remember to look at the scanner before he opened the doors. Now they're all gone. All gone. None of them could understand. Not even my little Susan, or Vicki. And as for Barbara and Chatterton – Chesterton. They were all too impatient to get back to their own time. And now, Steven. Perhaps I should go home, back to my own planet. But I can't. I can't.'

THE DOCTOR, *THE MASSACRE*

'That's right, yes, you're going. Been gone for ages. Already gone, still here, just arrived, haven't even met you yet. It all depends on who you are and how you look at it. Strange business, time ... Think about me when you're living your life one day after another, all in a neat pattern. Think about the homeless traveller and his old police box, his days like crazy paving.'

THE DOCTOR, *DRAGONFIRE*

SARAH: Don't forget me.

THE DOCTOR: Oh, Sarah. Don't you forget me.

SARAH: Bye, Doctor. You know, travel does broaden the mind.

THE DOCTOR: Yes. Till we meet again, Sarah.

THE HAND OF FEAR

SARAH: Goodbye, Doctor.

THE DOCTOR: Oh, it's not goodbye.

SARAH: Do say it. Please. This time. Say it.

THE DOCTOR: Goodbye, my Sarah Jane.

SCHOOL REUNION

'If you want to remember me, then you can do one thing. That's all, one thing. Have a good life. Do that for me, Rose. Have a fantastic life.'

THE DOCTOR, *THE PARTING OF THE WAYS*

'One day, I shall come back. Yes, I shall come back. Until then, there must be no regrets, no tears, no anxieties. Just go forward in all your beliefs, and prove to me that I am not mistaken in mine. Goodbye, Susan. Goodbye, my dear.'

THE DOCTOR, *THE DALEK INVASION OF EARTH*

THE DESTINY OF THE DOCTOR

'On the Fields of Trenzalore, at the fall of the Eleventh, when no living creature can speak falsely, or fail to answer, a question will be asked. A question that must never, ever be answered.'

DORIUM MALDOVAR, *THE WEDDING OF RIVER SONG*

RIVER: There are so many theories about you and I, you know.

THE DOCTOR: Idle gossip.

RIVER: Archaeology.

THE DOCTOR: Same thing.

THE WEDDING OF RIVER SONG

THE DOCTOR: You didn't listen, did you? You lot never do. That's the problem. The Doctor has a secret he will take to the grave. It is discovered. He wasn't talking about my secret. No, no, no, that's not what's been found. He was talking about my grave. Trenzalore is where I'm buried.

CLARA: How can you have a grave?

THE DOCTOR: Because we all do, somewhere out there in the future, waiting for us.

THE NAME OF THE DOCTOR

'So many secrets, Doctor. I'll help you keep them, of course ... but you're a fool nonetheless. It's all still waiting for you. The fields of Trenzalore, the fall of the Eleventh, and the question ... The first question. The question that must never be answered, hidden in plain sight. The question you've been running from all your life. Doctor who? Doctor who? Doctor who?'

DORIUM MALDOVAR, *THE WEDDING OF RIVER SONG*

THE ELEVENTH DOCTOR: I saw Trenzalore, where we're buried. We die in battle among millions.

THE TENTH DOCTOR: That's not how it's supposed to be.

THE ELEVENTH DOCTOR: That's where the story ends. Nothing we can do about it. Trenzalore is where you're going.

THE TENTH DOCTOR: Oh, never say nothing. Anyway, good to know my future is in safe hands.

THE DAY OF THE DOCTOR

'OK, so that's where I end up. Always thought maybe I'd retire. Take up watercolours or bee-keeping, or something. Apparently not.'

THE DOCTOR, *THE NAME OF THE DOCTOR*

THE DOCTOR: I could be a curator. I'd be great at curating. I'd be the great curator. I could retire and do that. I could retire and be the curator of this place.

THE CURATOR: You know, I really think you might.

THE DAY OF THE DOCTOR

THE DOCTOR: I never forget a face.

THE CURATOR: I know you don't. And in years to come, you might find yourself revisiting a few. But just the old favourites, eh?

THE DAY OF THE DOCTOR

THE TENTH DOCTOR: Trenzalore. We need a new destination because I don't want to go.

THE ELEVENTH DOCTOR: He always says that.

THE DAY OF THE DOCTOR

'Clara sometimes asks me if I dream. Of course I dream, I tell her. Everybody dreams. But what do you dream about, she'll ask. The same thing everybody dreams about, I tell her. I dream about where I'm going. She always laughs at that. But you're not going anywhere, you're just wandering about. That's not true. Not any more. I have a new destination. My journey is the same as yours, the same as anyone's. It's taken me so many years, so many lifetimes, but at last I know where I'm going. Where I've always been going. Home, the long way round.'

THE DOCTOR, *THE DAY OF THE DOCTOR*

FAMOUS LAST WORDS

(WELL, THE ONES WE HEARD ANYWAY)

'Ah, yes! Thank you. It's good. Keep warm.'

THE FIRST DOCTOR, *THE TENTH PLANET*

'No! Stop! You're making me giddy! No, you can't do this to me! No, no, no, no, no, no, no, no no, no, no, no, no…'

THE SECOND DOCTOR, *THE WAR GAMES*

'A tear, Sarah Jane? No don't cry. While there's life, there's...'

THE THIRD DOCTOR, *PLANET OF THE SPIDERS*

'It's the end, but the moment has been prepared for.'

THE FOURTH DOCTOR, *LOGOPOLIS*

'Might regenerate. I don't know. Feels different this time... Adric?'

THE FIFTH DOCTOR, *THE CAVES OF ANDROZANI*

'Carrot juice, carrot juice, carrot juice.'

THE SIXTH DOCTOR, *THE TRIAL OF A TIME LORD: THE ULTIMATE FOE*

'I've got to stop him.'

THE SEVENTH DOCTOR, *DOCTOR WHO* (TV MOVIE)

'Physician, heal thyself.'

THE EIGHTH DOCTOR, *THE NIGHT OF THE DOCTOR*

'Oh yes, of course. I suppose it makes sense. Wearing a bit thin. I hope the ears are a bit less conspicuous this time.'

THE WAR DOCTOR, *THE DAY OF THE DOCTOR*

'Rose, before I go, I just want to tell you, you were fantastic. Absolutely fantastic. And do you know what? So was I.'

THE NINTH DOCTOR, *THE PARTING OF THE WAYS*

'I don't want to go.'

THE TENTH DOCTOR, *THE END OF TIME*

'We all change, when you think about it. We're all different people all through our lives. And that's OK, that's good – you've gotta keep moving, so long as you remember all the people that you used to be. I will not forget one line of this. Not one day. I swear. I will always remember when the Doctor was me … Hey.'

THE ELEVENTH DOCTOR, *THE TIME OF THE DOCTOR*

APPENDIX

Credit must be given to the many writers and script editors who have put words in the mouths of the Doctor and his friends and enemies over the years. This book is dedicated to each and every one.

WRITERS

Ben Aaronovitch
REMEMBRANCE OF THE DALEKS, BATTLEFIELD

Douglas Adams
THE PIRATE PLANET, CITY OF DEATH (WITH GRAHAM WILLIAMS, AS DAVID AGNEW, FROM A STORY BY DAVID FISHER), SHADA

Christopher Bailey
KINDA, SNAKEDANCE

Bob Baker
NIGHTMARE OF EDEN

Bob Baker and Dave Martin
THE CLAWS OF AXOS, THE MUTANTS, THE THREE DOCTORS, THE SONTARAN EXPERIMENT, THE HAND OF FEAR, THE INVISIBLE ENEMY, UNDERWORLD, THE ARMAGEDDON FACTOR

Pip and Jane Baker
THE MARK OF THE RANI, THE TRIAL OF A TIME LORD: TERROR OF THE VERVOIDS, THE TRIAL OF A TIME LORD: THE ULTIMATE FOE (PART 14), TIME AND THE RANI

Christopher H. Bidmead
LOGOPOLIS, CASTROVALVA, FRONTIOS

Ian Stuart Black
*THE SAVAGES, THE WAR MACHINES
(FROM AN IDEA BY KIT PEDLER),
THE MACRA TERROR*

Chris Boucher
*THE FACE OF EVIL, THE ROBOTS OF
DEATH, IMAGE OF THE FENDAHL*

Ian Briggs
DRAGONFIRE, THE CURSE OF FENRIC

Johnny Byrne
*THE KEEPER OF TRAKEN,
ARC OF INFINITY, WARRIORS OF
THE DEEP*

Chris Chibnall
*42, THE HUNGRY EARTH / COLD
BLOOD, POND LIFE, DINOSAURS
ON A SPACESHIP, THE POWER OF
THREE*

Kevin Clarke
SILVER NEMESIS

Barbara Clegg
ENLIGHTENMENT

Anthony Coburn
AN UNEARTHLY CHILD

Paul Cornell
*FATHER'S DAY, HUMAN NATURE /
THE FAMILY OF BLOOD*

Donald Cotton
*THE MYTH MAKERS, THE
GUNFIGHTERS*

Neil Cross
THE RINGS OF AKHATEN, HIDE

Graeme Curry
THE HAPPINESS PATROL

Richard Curtis
VINCENT AND THE DOCTOR

Russell T Davies
*ROSE, THE END OF THE WORLD,
ALIENS OF LONDON / WORLD WAR
THREE, THE LONG GAME, BOOM
TOWN, BAD WOLF / THE PARTING
OF THE WAYS, BORN AGAIN,
THE CHRISTMAS INVASION, NEW
EARTH, TOOTH AND CLAW, LOVE
& MONSTERS, ARMY OF GHOSTS /
DOOMSDAY, THE RUNAWAY BRIDE,
SMITH AND JONES, GRIDLOCK,
UTOPIA, THE SOUND OF DRUMS /
LAST OF THE TIME LORDS, VOYAGE OF
THE DAMNED, PARTNERS IN CRIME,
MIDNIGHT, TURN LEFT, THE STOLEN
EARTH / JOURNEY'S END, THE NEXT
DOCTOR, THE END OF TIME, PART
ONE, THE END OF TIME, PART TWO*

**Russell T Davies
and Phil Ford**
THE WATERS OF MARS

**Russell T Davies
and Gareth Roberts**
PLANET OF THE DEAD

Gerry Davis
REVENGE OF THE CYBERMEN

Terrance Dicks
ROBOT, HORROR OF FANG ROCK,
STATE OF DECAY, THE FIVE DOCTORS

**Terrance Dicks
and Malcolm Hulke**
THE WAR GAMES

**Terrance Dicks
and Robert Holmes
(as Robin Bland)**
THE BRAIN OF MORBIUS

Terence Dudley
FOUR TO DOOMSDAY, BLACK ORCHID,
THE KING'S DEMONS

**David Ellis
and Malcolm Hulke**
THE FACELESS ONES

William Emms
GALAXY 4

**Paul Erickson
and Lesley Scott**
THE ARK

David Fisher
THE STONES OF BLOOD, THE
ANDROIDS OF TARA, THE CREATURE
FROM THE PIT, THE LEISURE HIVE

**John Flanagan and
Andrew McCulloch**
MEGLOS

Neil Gaiman
THE DOCTOR'S WIFE, NIGHTMARE
IN SILVER

Steve Gallagher
WARRIORS' GATE, TERMINUS

Mark Gatiss
THE UNQUIET DEAD, THE IDIOT'S
LANTERN, VICTORY OF THE DALEKS,
NIGHT TERRORS, COLD WAR,
THE CRIMSON HORROR

Matthew Graham
FEAR HER, THE REBEL FLESH /
THE ALMOST PEOPLE

Stephen Greenhorn
THE LAZARUS EXPERIMENT,
THE DOCTOR'S DAUGHTER

Peter Grimwade
TIME-FLIGHT, MAWDRYN UNDEAD,
PLANET OF FIRE

Mervyn Haisman
and Henry Lincoln
THE ABOMINABLE SNOWMEN, THE
WEB OF FEAR, THE DOMINATORS
(AS NORMAN ASHBY)

Brian Hayles
THE CELESTIAL TOYMAKER,
THE SMUGGLERS, THE ICE
WARRIORS, THE SEEDS OF DEATH,
THE CURSE OF PELADON, THE
MONSTER OF PELADON

Robert Holmes
THE KROTONS, THE SPACE PIRATES,
SPEARHEAD FROM SPACE,
TERROR OF THE AUTONS, CARNIVAL
OF MONSTERS, THE TIME WARRIOR,
THE ARK IN SPACE, PYRAMIDS OF
MARS (AS STEPHEN HARRIS),
THE DEADLY ASSASSIN, THE TALONS
OF WENG-CHIANG, THE SUN
MAKERS, THE RIBOS OPERATION, THE
POWER OF KROLL, THE CAVES OF
ANDROZANI, THE TWO DOCTORS,
THE TRIAL OF A TIME LORD: THE
MYSTERIOUS PLANET, THE TRIAL OF
A TIME LORD: THE ULTIMATE FOE
(PART 13)

Don Houghton
INFERNO, THE MIND OF EVIL

Malcolm Hulke
DOCTOR WHO AND THE SILURIANS,
COLONY IN SPACE, THE SEA DEVILS,
FRONTIER IN SPACE, INVASION OF
THE DINOSAURS

Matthew Jacobs
DOCTOR WHO (TV MOVIE)

Elwyn Jones
and Gerry Davis
THE HIGHLANDERS

Glyn Jones
THE SPACE MUSEUM

Matt Jones
THE IMPOSSIBLE PLANET /
THE SATAN PIT

Malcolm Kohll
DELTA AND THE BANNERMEN

Peter Ling
THE MIND ROBBER

John Lucarotti
MARCO POLO, THE AZTECS, THE
MASSACRE (FOURTH EPISODE
WITH DONALD TOSH)

Tom MacRae
RISE OF THE CYBERMEN / THE AGE OF STEEL, THE GIRL WHO WAITED

Louis Marks
PLANET OF GIANTS, DAY OF THE DALEKS, PLANET OF EVIL, THE MASQUE OF MANDRAGORA

Philip Martin
VENGEANCE ON VAROS, THE TRIAL OF A TIME LORD: MINDWARP

Glen McCoy
TIMELASH

Steven Moffat
THE EMPTY CHILD / THE DOCTOR DANCES, THE GIRL IN THE FIREPLACE, BLINK, TIME CRASH, SILENCE IN THE LIBRARY / FOREST OF THE DEAD, THE ELEVENTH HOUR, THE BEAST BELOW, THE TIME OF ANGELS / FLESH AND STONE, THE PANDORICA OPENS / THE BIG BANG, A CHRISTMAS CAROL, SPACE / TIME, THE IMPOSSIBLE ASTRONAUT / DAY OF THE MOON, A GOOD MAN GOES TO WAR, LET'S KILL HITLER, THE WEDDING OF RIVER SONG, THE DOCTOR, THE WIDOW AND THE WARDROBE, ASYLUM OF THE DALEKS, THE ANGELS TAKE MANHATTAN, THE SNOWMEN, THE BELLS OF SAINT JOHN, THE NAME OF THE DOCTOR, THE NIGHT OF THE DOCTOR, THE DAY OF THE DOCTOR, THE TIME OF THE DOCTOR

Paula Moore
ATTACK OF THE CYBERMEN

James Moran
THE FIRES OF POMPEII

Rona Munro
SURVIVAL

Terry Nation
THE DALEKS, THE KEYS OF MARINUS, THE DALEK INVASION OF EARTH, THE CHASE, MISSION TO THE UNKNOWN, THE DALEKS' MASTER PLAN (WITH DENNIS SPOONER), PLANET OF THE DALEKS, DEATH TO THE DALEKS, GENESIS OF THE DALEKS, THE ANDROID INVASION, DESTINY OF THE DALEKS

Peter R. Newman
THE SENSORITES

Simon Nye
AMY'S CHOICE

Geoffrey Orme
THE UNDERWATER MENACE

Kit Pedler
THE MOONBASE

**Kit Pedler
and Gerry Davis**
*THE TENTH PLANET, THE TOMB OF
THE CYBERMEN*

Victor Pemberton
FURY FROM THE DEEP

Marc Platt
GHOST LIGHT

Eric Pringle
THE AWAKENING

Helen Raynor
*DALEKS IN MANHATTAN /
EVOLUTION OF THE DALEKS,
THE SONTARAN STRATAGEM /
THE POISON SKY*

Anthony Read
THE HORNS OF NIMON

Gareth Roberts
*THE SHAKESPEARE CODE,
THE UNICORN AND THE WASP,
THE LODGER, CLOSING TIME*

Eric Saward
*THE VISITATION, EARTHSHOCK,
RESURRECTION OF THE DALEKS,
REVELATION OF THE DALEKS*

Robert Shearman
DALEK

Derrick Sherwin
*THE INVASION (FROM A STORY BY
KIT PEDLER)*

Robert Sloman
*THE DAEMONS (WITH BARRY
LETTS, AS GUY LEOPOLD), THE
TIME MONSTER, THE GREEN DEATH,
PLANET OF THE SPIDERS*

Andrew Smith
FULL CIRCLE

Dennis Spooner
*THE REIGN OF TERROR, THE
ROMANS, THE TIME MEDDLER,
THE DALEKS' MASTER PLAN (WITH
TERRY NATION)*

Anthony Steven
THE TWIN DILEMMA

Robert Banks Stewart
*TERROR OF THE ZYGONS,
THE SEEDS OF DOOM*

Bill Strutton
THE WEB PLANET

Keith Temple
PLANET OF THE OOD

Stephen Thompson
*THE CURSE OF THE BLACK SPOT,
JOURNEY TO THE CENTRE OF THE
TARDIS*

David Whitaker
*THE EDGE OF DESTRUCTION, THE
RESCUE, THE CRUSADE, THE POWER
OF THE DALEKS, THE EVIL OF THE
DALEKS, THE ENEMY OF THE WORLD,
THE WHEEL IN SPACE* (FROM A
STORY BY KIT PEDLER), *THE
AMBASSADORS OF DEATH*

Toby Whithouse
*SCHOOL REUNION, THE VAMPIRES
OF VENICE, THE GOD COMPLEX,
A TOWN CALLED MERCY*

Stephen Wyatt
*PARADISE TOWERS, THE GREATEST
SHOW IN THE GALAXY*

SCRIPT EDITORS

Douglas Adams
Lindsey Alford
Christopher H.
Bidmead
Peter Bryant
Andrew Cartmel
Richard Cookson
Gerry Davis
Terrance Dicks
Emma Freud

Caroline Henry
Robert Holmes
Brian Minchin
Victor Pemberton
John Phillips
Helen Raynor
Anthony Read
Derek Ritchie
Antony Root
Elwen Rowlands

Gary Russell
Eric Saward
Derrick Sherwin
Nikki Smith
Dennis Spooner
Donald Tosh
David Whitaker
Simon Winstone

THANKS

As always, there are people we must thank for their help, encouragement and support throughout the compiling of this book. Without whom...

The team at *Doctor Who Magazine* – Tom Spilsbury, Peter Ware, Richard Atkinson, John Ainsworth and Scott Gray.

Ben Morris, whose illustrations never cease to take our breath away when a new one drops into our inboxes.

A very special thanks to Daniel Brennan for his continued support, and being an eagle-eared knight in shining armour.

As always, the team at BBC Books who always make a new commission such a pleasurable experience. So to Albert DePetrillo for asking us back, Lizzy Gaisford for keeping us in check (and giving us Christmas!), and the ever-vigilant Justin Richards and Steve Tribe.

And finally, our families for love, support and cups of tea. For Cav – Clare, and his new little *Doctor Who* fans, Chloe and Connie. For Mark – Paula and Oliver.

INDEX

Doctor Dances, The 55, 57, 66, 67, 68, 70, 149, 203, 205, 268

Doctor, the Widow and the Wardrobe, The 7, 54, 56, 62, 63, 144, 272, 276, 277, 311

Doctor Who (TV Movie) 4, 131, 132, 148, 216, 294, 303, 311, 328

Doctor Who and the Silurians 20, 100, 228

Doctor's Daughter, The 11

Doctor's name, the 5–7

Doctor's Wife, The 17, 18, 38, 72, 79, 87, 92, 172, 176, 177

Dominators, The 138

Doomsday 123, 127, 128, 204

Dortmun 135, 265

Dragonfire 138, 156, 181, 227, 243, 322

Drathro 212, 214, 230

Droxil 56

Duggan 107, 152, 237, 259

Earth 12, 111, 153–4, 174, 264

Earthshock 59, 230, 236, 259

Edge of Destruction, The 58, 112, 143, 242

Editor, the 250

Einstein, Albert 276

INDEX